TRUE

MYSTERY

STORIES

TRUE MYSTERY STORIES

Terry Deary

Illustrated by

David Wyatt

■SCHOLASTIC

To Josh Fell

The facts behind these stories are true. However, they
have been dramatized to make them into gripping
stories, and some of the characters are fictitious.

Scholastic Children's Books,
Commonwealth House, 1-19 New Oxford Street,
London WC1A 1NU, UK

A division of Scholastic Ltd
London ~ New York ~ Toronto ~ Sydney ~ Auckland
Mexico City ~ New Delhi ~ Hong Kong

First published in the UK by Scholastic Ltd, 2000

Text copyright © Terry Deary, 2000
Illustrations copyright © David Wyatt, 2000

ISBN 0 439 01437 9

All rights reserved

Typeset by TW Typesetting, Midsomer Norton, Somerset
Printed by Cox & Wyman, Reading, Berks

10 9 8 7 6 5 4 3 2 1

CONTENTS

INTRODUCTION

The world is full of mysteries. It always has been. Before people could write they looked up at the sky and wondered where the Sun went every night … then they solved the "mystery" by explaining that it was pulled across the sky in a chariot and disappeared under the flat Earth.

Scientists have come along with a better explanation of course, and that particular mystery has been solved. But it doesn't matter how clever human beings become, there will always be some things we can't explain. Some old mysteries will stay unsolved for ever, though with others we can have a good guess at the truth.

We love mysteries the way we love puzzles. But mysteries can also give us shivers the way a good thriller story can. The trouble is, it's not always so much fun being near the centre of a mystery.

Two days before sitting down to write this I was in an old hall in Chepstow, on the Welsh border with England. I was due to perform a show in which I'd tell stories, recite poems and sing songs, all to do with history.

The organizer suddenly asked, "You won't be doing anything about the First World War, will you?"

"Yes," I told her. "I do three songs, a poem and a couple of stories. Why?"

She shrugged, "It's just … you may have trouble with the ghost."

"You are joking?" I laughed.

She shook her head slowly and explained. "Last year we had an actor in the hall. He was doing a play about the First World War and he was dressed in full uniform. Half an hour before the show was due to start I was having tea in the snack bar when the actor walked in and asked me, 'Who is the old guy in the uniform?' I shook my head. 'There aren't any old guys in uniform – except you.' The actor frowned and said, 'I stepped out of the dressing room at the back of the stage and an old man walked past me. He was in a First World War uniform and he had a chest full of medal ribbons. I thought you must have invited him to watch the show. I couldn't have imagined it!' We went to the back of the stage and searched it from end to end. There was no old man in uniform – there was no one at all."

"So you're telling me there's a ghost haunting this hall who only appears when someone turns up as a First World War character?" I asked the organizer.

She shrugged again. "It looks that way," she said. "Though there are reports of other ghosts that haunt this hall."

"Thanks, mate," I muttered as I tried to prepare myself for the show. A hundred and fifty people took their seats and I began.

The Romans and the Middle Ages were fine. The Tudors and the Victorians were no problem. Then I reached the First World War section. I'd like to tell you how I sang "Pack up your troubles", how I looked over the heads of the audience and there – standing at the back of the room – was an old man in a First World War uniform.

But I can't tell you that because it didn't happen. The ghost didn't show up that night. That doesn't prove he doesn't exist … Her Majesty the Queen didn't show up that night either, but that doesn't prove *she* doesn't exist. Maybe the ghost (like the Queen) isn't a fan!

Can you explain this story and solve the mystery? Perhaps the actor was deceived by a trick of the light – maybe he walked past a mirror by the door and saw his own reflection!

Maybe he made up the story and told the organizer a lie just as a joke. Maybe the organizer made it up and told me a lie just to scare me! Maybe I made it up and I am telling you this lie because it is a good way to introduce a book on mysteries! (But I'm not.)

Mistakes, jokes, scary stories and downright lies. They can all be used to explain some stories.

Then there are other sorts of mystery – like the mystery of how ships and aircraft seem to disappear in one part of the world's oceans – and crime and murder mysteries. There are unexplained disappearances … as well as unexplained appearances – lights in the sky that move too fast to be anything human. There are mysteries of strange human powers that seem impossible – but really happened.

This book will look at just a few of the billions of mysteries that have happened through human history. The mysteries will be told as stories; they are "true" because someone at some time has said they happened. There will be fact files to help you make up your own mind or to help you solve the mystery where it is possible.

Will you be able to? Who knows? It's a mystery.

WHAT HAPPENED TO MRS GREAVES?

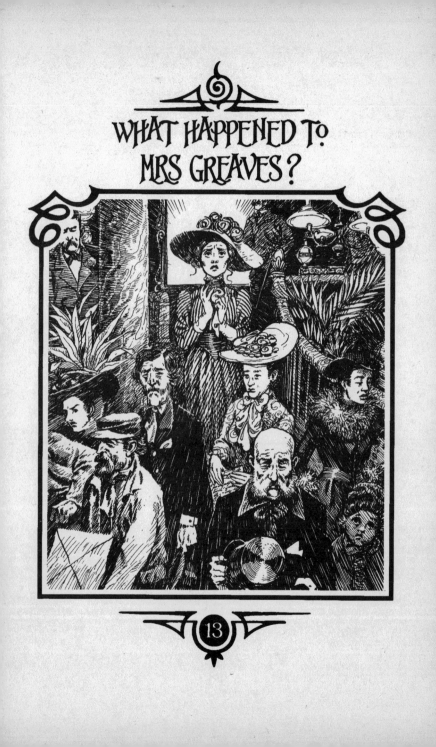

Some mysteries have never been solved. But, if you think about it, there may be an explanation for the most unlikely events. Take the terrible tale of a young woman who went mad because she couldn't solve the mystery of her disappearing mother...

Paris, May 1889

The British ambassador was a grey man. He wore a black coat and a dove-grey waistcoat. His perfectly creased trousers and silver hair, his pale eyes behind rimless spectacles, were just as colourless. Even his skin was grey in the early evening light.

He sat behind a massive desk in the richly decorated room and he sighed. "It's the end of the day, Bentley," he murmured to the young, shrunken man who stood in front of him. "I am tired. Tell the woman I'll see her tomorrow."

Bentley raised a thin hand and coughed into it. "She insists. She won't go away, Your Excellency. She is frantic, hysterical."

The ambassador removed his spectacles and rubbed his eyes wearily. When he looked up his eyes were cold and hard. "Bentley."

"Your Excellency?"

"Get rid of her!"

The secretary bowed. He was as colourless as his master except for the fair hair that flopped forward as he bowed again and backed towards the door. Just as he reached it the door burst open and a woman rushed in. She was as colourful as the men were grey. Her red hair was tumbling free from the green hat that matched her eyes. Her satin dress was striped green and purple and there were red spots of anger on her pink cheeks.

"Young lady..." the ambassador began.

She didn't let him finish. "I am Alice Greaves. I hold a

British passport. You are a servant of Her Majesty Queen Victoria and it is your duty to help me."

The ambassador froze. "I have a dinner appointment with the President of France this evening. Her Majesty would not want me to miss it. *That* is my first duty." He strode towards the open door and as he walked he said, "Bentley here will deal with you." Then he was gone into the darkening corridors.

The secretary with the floppy fair hair wrung his pale hands then waved one at a rich velvet chair. "Please, sit down Miss Greaves. Please. I am Andrew Bentley. May I get you a glass of water?"

Alice ignored the offer. "This is a matter of life and death. We arrived in Paris last night and we went straight from the railway station to the Hôtel Parnasse…"

The young man held a glass of water in front of her and said quietly. "Start at the beginning, Miss Greaves. Where had you come from?"

"From India. My father manages a tea company and we went to India to spend the winter with him."

"We?"

"Mother and I," she explained. She pushed a strand of hair back under her hat and took a sip of the water. "Mother is not a strong woman. We decided it would be better for her to avoid the winter in England."

The secretary nodded. His face was not so ugly when he smiled and his eyes were kind. "You must have arrived on the 5:30 train from Marseilles this evening." She nodded. "You went to the hotel. What happened then?"

Alice Greaves bit her lip. "Mother had been ill on the train. We thought the railway would be better than taking a ship. The voyage out to India almost killed her. But the train journey was no better. She was so weak I could barely get her into the room. I hoped that a rest in the hotel would do her good."

"But she grew worse?"

"Much worse!" Alice groaned. "She had a fever. She was awake but crying out in terror as if she was having nightmares. It wasn't travel sickness. It was something much worse."

Andrew Bentley nodded slowly. "Of course, the hotel got a doctor for you?"

"Of course. Doctor Raoul, I think he said. I wasn't paying much attention. The manager of the Hôtel Parnasse sent for him. The doctor seemed to know what he was doing, but my French is not very good. He had a lot to say to the manager but very little to me. He bathed mother's forehead with cold water then he turned to me and said he wanted me to fetch medicine for her."

The secretary frowned. "Why send *you*? A stranger in the city? Why couldn't the hotel send a porter?"

The girl shrugged. "I never thought of that at the time. But the doctor wrote the name of the medicine on a scrap of paper and an address. Then they told me to take a cab."

"Was it far?" the secretary asked. Alice Greaves handed him the crumpled slip of paper. He raised his fair eyebrows. "About as far away from the hotel as you could get! There are chemists much closer. Maybe this is some special medicine," he murmured.

"It took me two hours to get there, wait for the medicine to be mixed, and get back," she sighed and rustled restlessly in the satin dress.

"And the medicine didn't work?" Andrew asked. "You want a British doctor to examine her?"

She shook her head sharply and red hair fell loose again. "Oh, no, Mr Bentley. It is worse than that. Much, much worse than that! When I returned to the hotel my mother had vanished!"

The young man's mouth fell open. "She'd packed and left?"

"No. I mean it was as if she had never been there. The bed looked as though it had never been disturbed. My bags were in the room, but hers were gone … and so was she."

Andrew Bentley took a deep breath and his rounded back almost straightened. "What did the manager say?"

Alice's green eyes turned towards him. Her cheeks were pale now, her voice a little hoarse. "That's the horrible thing! The manager said my mother had never been there! He said I had arrived alone and I had left earlier in a cab alone."

"Her name would be in the hotel register," the secretary pointed out gently. "It is the law of France. All guests must sign in the register."

"Mother was too *ill* to sign. I just signed myself in then helped her up to the room. Room 215 on the second floor."

Andrew took the glass of water from her hand and put it on a table. "I think I should go to the hotel with you," he said.

"Would you?"

"Of course," he said, and gave the same nervous little bow that he gave to the ambassador.

They left the embassy in a cab and clattered through the cobbled streets of Paris. Gas street lamps were being lit across the city. People strolled through the mild spring evening and chattered. But in the cab there was a grim silence.

When they pushed through the heavy hotel doors the manager stepped out smartly from behind the desk. "Monsieur?" he asked.

"My name's Bentley, and I'm from the British Embassy," Andrew said as firmly as his soft voice would allow. "I've come to investigate Miss Greaves's complaint about her mother."

The manager's frown faded and he smiled under his thin moustache. He took the young secretary by the arm and led him into a quiet corner of the entrance hall. He spoke quickly. "A sad case, monsieur! The young lady, she is completely mad! She came in alone and went out in a cab. She came back an hour later and said her mother was missing. We searched the room – we searched the hotel – but there was no sign of any old woman here!"

19

Andrew looked at the man. He sounded honest enough. For the first time the young man felt a flicker of doubt. "And the doctor ... Doctor Raoul?"

The manager shrugged one shoulder. "We do have a Doctor Raoul staying with us. He is here in the lounge, reading a book," he said and again took Andrew's arm to lead him.

Alice rushed past and dropped to her knees in front of a man with grey whiskers. "Doctor Raoul! You have to tell this man the truth! You saw my mother."

The man lowered the book slowly. "I am sorry, mademoiselle. I have never had the honour of meeting your mother."

Alice Greaves sank back on her heels as if he had slapped her. "You sent me for medicine!"

"You are mistaken."

She tore the scrap of paper from a pocket in her silk dress. "This is your note! You wrote it!"

The man opened the book and showed her the inside cover where he had written his name and address. "Excuse me, mademoiselle, but that is not my handwriting."

The young woman buried her face in her hands and groaned, "No, no, no!"

Andrew Bentley raised her gently to her feet and said, "Shall we look in the room?"

She moved wearily, helplessly to the door and into the cage of the lift. The manager chattered as it creaked and rumbled slowly upwards. "Perhaps mademoiselle is mistaken... Perhaps mademoiselle herself has been ill..."

When they reached room 215 the manager used a large key to unlock the door. For the first time since they'd left the doctor Alice looked up. She gave a small scream and stumbled forward. The bed was hung with dark red curtains and the covers were a shade of pink. "Look!" she cried.

"The bed is empty," Andrew said softly.

"The bedclothes, the drapes around the bed. They're *red*!" she said. "When I brought mother in they were *blue*. The hotel has changed them all!"

"Aha!" the manager cried happily. "That explains it! Mademoiselle, you are thinking of another hotel, another room, another city! See? I told you your mother was never here!"

Alice Greaves sobbed as if her heart was breaking. She clutched at one of the bed posts and moaned, "Mother!" over and over again.

It was another half an hour before Doctor Raoul could get her to take a potion that sent her to sleep. In another 15 minutes she had been strapped on to a stretcher and carried to the back entrance of the hotel.

It was dark by then. No one saw Alice loaded into the horse-drawn ambulance. Only a nurse and Doctor Raoul travelled with her on the Calais train and saw her safely on to the Channel boat to Dover.

The ambassador looked up from the papers on his desk. Andrew Bentley stood silently in front of the desk, more bent and shrunken than ever. "Whatever happened to that woman, Bentley? The one who barged in here screaming like a madwoman?"

"Poor lady's back in England, Your Excellency," the secretary sighed.

The ambassador peered at him through his spectacles. "Poor lady?"

Andrew raised a hand and coughed. "The French handed her straight over to our medical services. They've locked her away in a lunatic asylum, Your Excellency."

"Hah!" the ambassador barked. "I said she was a madwoman, didn't I? Mad as a dog. Lunatic asylum's the best place for people like that!"

The secretary didn't reply.

The ambassador looked up at him again. "Well, Bentley? If the French say she's mad, then she's mad."

"Perhaps, Your Excellency." It was almost a whisper.

"Something about a disappearing mother, wasn't it?" the man asked sharply.

"Yes, Excellency."

The ambassador waved a pen at his secretary. "Let me tell you, Bentley, women do not disappear into thin air. And if the young woman says she did then she's mad, take my word for it."

"Maybe losing her mother like that could have driven her mad," the secretary mumbled.

The ambassador threw the pen on the desk with a clatter and a tiny splash of ink. "You can *not* believe her, Bentley, surely! If the mother really existed then where did she go? Can you tell me?"

"No, Excellency," Andrew Bentley sighed. "It's a mystery. A mystery."

Solve the mystery

The British Embassy solved the mystery to their satisfaction –
they said that Alice Greaves was mad, and that she had made
up the story of her mother being in the hotel.

We can't talk to Alice to see if she is a truthful person. And
we can't check her story for ourselves. It *is* possible that Alice
imagined it. But what if Alice was telling the truth? Is there
another explanation that fits Alice's "facts"? According to
Alice...

- Mrs Greaves arrived at the hotel, alive but ill.
- The doctor examined her and sent Alice off for medicine.
- The doctor later denied he had ever seen Alice or her
  mother.
- Her mother had gone when Alice returned.
- The hotel manager denied that Mrs Greaves had arrived
  with Alice.
- The bedding in the room was changed.

Can you think of an explanation? Here is one that has been
put forward...

*Alice and her mother arrived at the hotel from India as Mrs Greaves
was dying. As soon as the doctor examined her he knew that the older
woman was suffering from a terrible disease picked up in India – a
plague, perhaps. If the guests at the hotel ever found out they would
flee, the hotel would be closed down and the staff would lose their jobs.*

*The doctor, a friend of the manager, sent Alice Greaves away for a
couple of hours. When the old woman died her corpse was bundled
into the bedclothes, pushed into a coffin and buried quickly in an
unmarked grave, somewhere in Paris.*

*The hotel manager destroyed the materials in the room where she
had died. They could have been carrying the disease. He had them
replaced along with fresh bedclothes. He also destroyed the suitcase and*

clothes that had arrived with the dead woman to be extra sure of not passing any germs on.

When Alice Greaves returned, the doctor and the hotel staff had all agreed to tell her that her mother had never been there. Alice was driven mad by the loss of her mother and was sent back to Britain with a story about her being mad. Alice insisted that her mother had vanished, so British doctors kept her locked away.

1. In the USA a mysterious disappearance is often called "pulling a Crater". This is because of what happened to Judge Joseph Crater on 6 August 1930. He stepped out of a New York nightclub and took a taxi to a theatre. He bought a ticket for a show called *Dancing Partners* ... and was never seen again, alive or dead. Police still have him listed as a missing person (though he'd be 100 years old by now) and they still get reports of him being sighted! There are a few clues to his mystery disappearance. He got an upsetting phone call at his home. Then he got his assistant to collect $8,000 cash from the bank. Perhaps Judge Crater simply had a problem and had to run away and hide.

2. In 1920 newspapers reported that the British Member of Parliament Victor Grayson had boarded the Hull train at Liverpool station. He never arrived. The mystery puzzled people for 20 years. They wondered how a man could vanish from a moving train. No body was found at the side of the tracks and no one saw him again. In fact, the "mystery" is not so mysterious after all. Grayson did *not* disappear from a train. He was last seen leaving his flat in

London – not boarding a train. He was collected by two men and took his suitcases with him. It seems he may have been in danger of going to jail. Did Victor Grayson simply "pull a Crater"?

3. A stranger disappearance happened in Australia in 1978. Frederick Valentich, the pilot of a light aircraft, reported that he was being tracked by a flying object the like of which he'd never seen before. His last radio message said, "That strange aircraft is hovering over me. It is hovering and it's not an aircraft…" Then there was silence. No wreckage was ever found. There had been a lot of sightings of Unidentified Flying Objects (UFOs) in that area. Many people believed Valentich and his plane had been kidnapped by aliens. But Valentich collected press cuttings on UFOs and was fascinated by them. Did he use the UFO stories as a cover for his own disappearance? One story reported that he was alive and well, working in a petrol station in Tasmania!

4. The famous woman pilot, Amelia Earhart disappeared as she flew across the Pacific Ocean. She was due to land for fuel on Howland Island but never arrived. Some investigators said that Amelia was flying over Japanese Islands and acting as a US spy. They blamed the Japanese for shooting her down. Recent reports say that parts of her plane and a shoe have been found on another island – she crash landed and was killed. This is far more likely. Howland Island is just half a mile wide – a tiny speck in an ocean thousands of miles wide. In cloudy conditions Amelia Earhart simply lost her way.

5. Amy Johnson was Britain's most famous woman flyer of the 1930s. Her disappearance is harder to explain. When war broke out she took a job delivering aircraft around Britain. She had flown to Australia so flying from Lancashire to Kidlington near Oxford on 5 January 1941 should have been no problem, in spite of the low cloud. At 3:30 p.m. a ship at the mouth of the Thames saw one or maybe two people parachute from a falling aircraft. One of the crew disappeared into the icy waters – too weak and cold to grasp the rescuers' ropes. A sailor swam out to save the second aircrew swimmer but he died from the cold before he reached them and no one else was found. A bag salvaged from the wreckage contained Amy Johnson's flying book. But she was flying alone! Who was the second mystery parachutist? And why was she 100 miles off course? There were rumours that she'd actually flown to France to collect a secret agent. It's a mystery. One possible answer is that she was running out of fuel and went to the back cargo hatch to bail out. The second shape the sailors saw through the mist was actually the door to the hatch.

WHO'S BURIED IN THE GRAVE OF THE DUKE?

Just as mysterious as disappearances are appearances. Appearances like that of the Duke of Perth, who died after the last great battle in Scotland … or did he?

Biddick, Durham, England, 1801

"When I grow up I'm going to be a coal miner, just like my dad," Henry Barron said. "I'll have big muscles like an ox and I'll drink lots of beer!" He was only ten years old but he was bigger than the other boys in the group. He turned his dark little eyes on the smallest boy. "What are you going to be, Thomas Drummond?"

The boy jumped. The eyes of all the other boys turned towards him. He hated that. Hated being noticed. His voice piped and cracked. "I'm going to be the Duke of Perth!" he said.

There was silence for a moment. Then the boys roared and sniggered and laughed till they cried. All the boys except Henry Barron, that was. He stared at Thomas and a sneer curled one nostril of his ugly, dirty face. "I was asking you a serious question, Thomas Drummond." The boys stopped laughing suddenly and stepped back. Henry Barron jabbed the small boy in the shoulder with a thick finger. "Don't try to be funny with me … or you know what you'll get?"

"No?" Thomas answered.

It was the wrong thing to say. Henry Barron's thick arm moved quickly and his hard fist smacked Thomas on the side of the head. The boys seemed to suck in their breaths together. Thomas blinked but sniffed quickly to stop the tears. "That's what you'll get … Your Grace!"

Thomas turned without a word and walked slowly away down the path by the River Wear, his head ringing like a cathedral bell. He walked past the little rowing boat that ferried people over the river and pushed open the door to the boatman's house.

A woman looked up from her needlework at the kitchen table as he walked in. He was glad it was his Aunt Elizabeth. She was always kind. She protected him like a mother hawk protects her chick in the woods by the river bank. "Hello, Thomas," she said. Her sharp eyes never left the boy's face.

"Hello, Auntie," he mumbled.

"Are you all right?" she asked.

"Auntie," he said, "Will you tell me again how I'm going to be Duke of Perth one day?" He bit his lip to stop the tears. When he was calmer he went on, "The boys don't believe me."

"Then they'll be sorry, won't they?" she said quietly. She took his skinny hand and pulled him over to her. She sat him on her knee and stroked his dark, dusty hair.

"Your grandfather, James Drummond, was the Duke of Perth," she began. The boy rested his head on her shoulder and listened to the familiar story. "He was a great soldier was James, Duke of Perth. Back in 1745 the great Bonnie Prince Charlie arrived on the coast of Scotland from his exile in France. He came with just a handful of men. He wanted to claim the British crown for his family."

"The Scottish lords met him and told him to go home!" Thomas said. "They told him he had no chance!"

"And Prince Charlie looked them in the eye and said, 'I am home! Scotland is my home!' Your grandfather was the first to kneel before him and kiss the prince's hand. 'I will fight for Your Highness and fight to the death!' he declared."

"But they lost," Thomas sighed.

"They fought against the mighty English army. They drove the English all the way to the Midlands! They could have marched on to London and taken the throne … but they turned back to Scotland. It was a terrible mistake, Thomas," the woman groaned.

"And then the English beat them, didn't they?"

"Oh, the English sent a great army to chase them through Scotland. They finally caught up with them at Culloden Moor, way up in the north. The poor Scots were starved by then. Some of them hadn't eaten for three days. But did that stop them from facing the English army?"

"No, Auntie!"

"No! They had swords and shields and hearts as big as oxen! But they had no armour and few guns. They faced the English Redcoats across the terrible moor and they charged at them! Charged at the English cannon, charged at the English

33

muskets! They screamed with hatred and even when the bullets flayed them they still kept charging! They were broken and shattered by the bullets and still they tried to go forward. The battlefield was red with their brave blood."

"Even my grandfather was wounded, wasn't he?" Thomas asked.

"He was hit in the cheek and hit in the hand. But he couldn't bear to see his gallant highlanders die like that. He called for them to retreat. The ones who were too slow were caught by the English and slaughtered on the ground where they fell. They called the English leader 'The Butcher'."

"But they didn't kill grandfather," Thomas said proudly.

"No, your grandfather hid in the woods. He hid through the terrible cold nights. He lay there and listened to the screams of the Scots as the English caught them and killed them. Then, after three days, he crept out and went down to the coast. That's where he found a small fishing boat that was willing to carry him away to safety. The rest of the leaders – like Bonnie Prince Charlie himself, had fled to France. But your gallant grandfather asked to be taken to the north of England! He was dropped off at the mouth of this very river!"

"He wasn't going to run away," Thomas said, and his chest swelled.

"It was a dangerous thing to do. There was a reward of £10,000 for his capture but he came to England and settled here in Biddick on the banks of the Wear. Maybe he would have formed a new army and fought the English again, but of course he met your grandmother – my mother – and fell in love with her."

"Was she beautiful?" Thomas asked.

"She was 16 years old when grandfather met her. She was as lovely as the Scottish heather, your grandfather always used to say. That's what kept him here. He took a job rowing the ferryboat and settled here."

"So who became Duke when my grandfather died?" Thomas asked.

"Why your father, of course! It always passes on to the oldest son," Aunt Elizabeth explained.

Thomas slipped from her knee and went to get a sugared plum from the jar in the larder. His aunt always let him have one. He stood in the doorway to the larder and frowned. "That's what I don't understand. If father is Duke of Perth then he owns castles and land and lots of gold."

"He does."

"So why does he go down the mine to dig coal every day?"

Aunt Elizabeth shrugged. "At first it was too dangerous to admit grandfather was the Duke. He'd have been executed. Then, when your grandfather died, ten years before you were born, my brother William took some family papers to London to make a claim. But William's ship was attacked by pirates. He was killed and the papers lost. And there was a flood on the river bank 12 years ago and the rest of our papers were washed away. Your father just gave up."

"So I'll never be Duke of Perth," Thomas sighed.

Aunt Elizabeth sucked in her pale cheeks. "You will, my boy, you *will*. The Duke's riches have been passed on to some young upstart called Captain James Drummond – he has the money, but he doesn't have the title! I went to see him in London last year and I met his wife. She as good as admitted your father is the Duke!"

"Can't we ever get our castles, Aunt Elizabeth?" Thomas said mournfully.

"One day, boy. One day. I have met a lawyer. A clever man. He says that even though your father doesn't care about the money and the titles, we can still make a claim for *you*. When you are old enough, Thomas, we will take this Captain to court! You will be Duke of Perth, Thomas."

Thomas rubbed the side of his sore face. "What do I tell Henry Barron and the boys, Auntie Elizabeth? When I tell them I'm going to be Duke of Perth they bully me."

The woman reached out and took his hand. She looked into his eyes and said, "Then tell them you are going to be a miner. It may be true for a while. But always remember my promise to you ... you may live like a poor miner's son, my young lord, but you will die a Duke! You mark my words ... you will die a Duke!"

Biddick, Durham, England, today

Go to All Saints Church in Penshaw, County Durham today. You can find it on a map. The graveyard has a path down the centre with railings either side. Walk down the path and look at the old gravestones carefully. You will come across a stone that is carved with the words:

The Burial Place of the Drummond Family.

The inscription on the green–black stone is a long one. You can see the names of eight children; six female and two male. Their mother Jane died in 1871 aged 77, and squeezed at the end, there it is:

Thomas Drummond the rightful heir to the Earldom of Perth who died November 1873 aged 81 years.

Little Thomas Drummond grew up and lived to the great old age of 81. He lived as a poor labourer with his wife and eight children. But he died, as his aunt had promised, as the Duke of Perth.

Was he?

Solve the mystery

When Thomas's father died in 1823, Thomas believed he was now Duke of Perth. With the help of his fierce Aunt Elizabeth he took his case to the highest courts in Britain.

In 1834 a court in Edinburgh listened to Thomas's case. They read a letter which mysteriously appeared just before the trial. It said:

To James Drummond at Biddick, County Durham

16 April 1747

Dear James

I think you had better come to France, where you would be out of danger, as I find you are living secretly at Biddick. You say it is reported that you died on your journey to France. If the English discover the truth they will have you executed.
Come to France.

Your brother,

John Drummond

The letter seemed to prove that the old Duke of Perth did NOT die after the battle of Culloden! He had survived, so his grandson must be the new Duke of Perth!

Amazing! But where had that letter been for nearly 90 years? Or was it a forgery?

If you had been a judge at Edinburgh what would *you* have decided? Look at the evidence:

Thomas Drummond IS NOT the Duke of Perth because...

- The old Duke was wounded at Culloden and there are several letters and diaries that say he fled on a ship to France with the other Scottish leaders. Those same letters say he died on the ship and was buried at sea. These people knew the old Duke and they saw him dead and buried.
- The old Duke had been brought up in France as a nobleman. He was 34 years old at the time of Culloden. Would a 34-year-old lord choose to marry a 16-year-old Durham miner's daughter?
- The Duke could have escaped to safety in France with the other losers. Would he choose to land in the very country where he'd be executed if he'd been discovered?
- A nobleman with a French accent would not take a job as a ferryboat man. Every traveller across the river (including soldiers and loyal English subjects) would notice him from his accent and his unusual manners. He would not last a week without being arrested.
- The old Duke would NOT have received that letter from his brother John. If John knew the Duke was hiding in Durham then so would the English government spies who opened and read all letters from France. If the English spies hadn't heard about this famous fugitive before then they would as soon as they opened the letter from his brother!
- The Biddick Duke's son (Thomas's father) never bothered to make a claim, even after it was safe for him to do so. He knew his father and he never believed the drunken stories about him being the Duke of Perth.

OR:

Thomas Drummond IS the Duke of Perth because...

- The old Duke survived the battle – this is proved by the letter.
- The old Duke's daughter (Elizabeth) SAYS he was the Duke.

Well? Which way would you vote? And which way did the Edinburgh judges vote?

The Edinburgh judges said that James Drummond *had* survived Culloden so Thomas Drummond *was* the Duke of Perth! *But* they also said that Captain Drummond's family had held the land for over 50 years so they could keep it. Thomas Drummond was a lord with no land.

Thomas died a poor Durham labourer ... but his gravestone still carried that proud claim: *Thomas Drummond the rightful heir to the Earldom of Perth.*

Of course, the Edinburgh judges may have got it wrong. Old James Drummond of Biddick *could* have been as phoney as that letter. But if he wasn't the real Duke of Perth, then who was he?

Can you think of an explanation? Here is one that has been put forward...

James Drummond, Duke of Perth, was wounded at the battle of Culloden and died on the ship going to France. One of his servants was also called James Drummond, because servants were often from the same clan as their lord. Servant James wasn't allowed on to the French boat – that was just for lords. He had to make his escape on a fishing boat and still had a few belongings of the Duke with him.

But that fishing boat just took him as far as the River Wear in County Durham and that is where he made a life for himself.

James Drummond the servant landed and married the 16-year-old miner's daughter and settled down with their children — no one was seeking him because no one cared about a humble serving man.

Their youngest daughter, Elizabeth, heard James Drummond boast about fighting at Culloden. Sometimes her father (a heavy drinker) told the tale as if he was the Duke. Elizabeth believed him. She in turn made her nephew Thomas believe it. The crafty lawyer forged a letter which seemed to show the Duke had not died. The Edinburgh court believed it and Thomas Drummond was declared Duke of Perth — but didn't get the Perth fortune.

Whenever there is a fortune to be made then a "dead" or missing person can suddenly turn up. And there always seems to be someone who believes that that person is the real one. Who knows, some of them may even be true…

1. Anastasia. Anastasia was the youngest daughter of Tsar Nicholas II of Russia. In July 1918 the whole family was assassinated in the Russian Revolution. In 1920 a woman was rescued from a Berlin canal.

She claimed to be Anastasia and said a guard had rescued her from the massacre. She adopted the name "Anna Anderson" and claimed the family fortune. The family lawyers said she was actually Franziska Shantkovska, a Polish bottle-factory worker. "Anna Anderson" died in 1984.

Modern scientific tests can tell if she was Anastasia or Franziska. They prove that she was Franziska. But many people refuse to believe the tests and insist she was the Russian princess.

2. Prince Louis Charles. In 1789 the French Revolution began. The Royal family were imprisoned and in 1793 King Louis XVI of France was beheaded on the guillotine. But his son, Prince Louis Charles, was left to rot in prison. He was said to have died in 1795, at the age of ten, from disease and neglect. He was buried in a local graveyard. There were many stories that said a dead peasant child had been placed in the coffin and Louis Charles had escaped. In the next 30 years 40 men turned up claiming to be the dead prince! One man, Karl Naundorff, was recognized by one of the jailers and spent many years trying to claim Louis Charles' throne. Prince Louis Charles' sister refused to see the man, yet when he died in 1845 she was sent a painting of the man on his deathbed and she was very upset. Why? Because she suspected it really was her brother who had died … a second time?

3. Joan of Arc. A French peasant girl, Joan of Arc, led the French to victory over the English invaders. In time the English captured her and had her tried for witchcraft. They sentenced her to die as a witch – tied to a stake and burned alive in 1431. Her greatest victory had been at

Orleans in 1428 where she was a heroine. Still, the people of Orleans were amazed to see her return in 1436 … five years after she'd been burned to death! They gave her lots of money. Some say that Joan escaped burning – another woman took her place at the stake. Others say the second Joan was a fake – someone who looked like the dead Joan. It may even have been her own sister trying to cash in on Joan's fame.

4. Kasper Hauser. A teenage boy wandered into Nuremberg, Germany, in 1826 and claimed that he'd spent years as a prisoner. His name, scrawled on a piece of paper, was Kasper Hauser. Young Kasper came to the notice of a lawyer who claimed the boy was the rightful heir to the royal Baden fortunes. Before he could prove it the lawyer died. The public was losing interest in the case when Kasper staggered into his teacher's house, bleeding from stab wounds.

He said he'd been set on by a masked attacker – many people believed he'd stabbed himself to get more attention for his case. Kasper died a few days later still claiming, "I didn't do it to myself." Who he was and how he died will remain a mystery. There is one interesting clue. The doctor said Kasper was stabbed by a left-handed man – and Kasper was left-handed.

5. Prince Richard. Making a sudden appearance from the dead can be a dangerous business. Two English princes almost certainly died in the Tower of London in 1483, perhaps murdered on the orders of their uncle, King Richard III. The younger boy, Richard, turned up eight years later and claimed his family fortune. He found many followers in Ireland and Scotland and tried to lead an invasion against King Henry VII. He was arrested and, after trying to escape, he was executed in the Tower. So Prince Richard died in the Tower of London … twice!

FACT·FILE

H0W DID FLIGHT 19 VANISH?

People are fascinated by mysteries. But some stories become confused and change as they are told over and over again. In time the truth is lost. Take the famous mystery of the Hoodoo Sea, the Graveyard of the Atlantic, the Sea of Lost Ships and the Devil's triangle. Where are these places? They are all the same place – probably best-known as the Bermuda Triangle…

The west Atlantic Ocean

The skipper of the fishing boat scratched his grey beard and yawned. The sea was flat as a mill pond, the fish were not biting on the bait and the fishermen were bored.

The fat American in the bright yellow shirt and turquoise shorts turned to the skipper. "Hey, bud. This is a waste of time! We hired this boat so you could take us to where the best fishing is! This is costing us a hundred bucks a day … each! If I catch nothing I want my hundred bucks back."

The skipper took a deep breath. His tanned face was hard as leather and he hid his disgust easily. "Sorry about that, sir. I guess the curse is working today. Some days the fish just leap out of the water at you. But when the triangle does its magic then the fish go down deep and hide."

The little fisherman with the big white baseball cap spoke in a piping voice. "Hey! That's right, Hank! We're off the coast of Miami!"

His fat friend sneered, "I know where we are Chuck – the skipper here may be lost but I'm not. We're 50 miles due east of Fort Lauderdale."

"No!" the little fisherman cried. "I mean we're slap bang in the middle of the Bermuda Triangle! Hey, Hank! If the force is on us we may not even get back safely!"

Fat Hank mopped his brow with a handkerchief and tried

not to sound too bothered. "We're not in any danger, are we skipper? You've sailed these waters for 50 years, you told us. You've never had any problems."

The old skipper sucked his teeth and was slow to reply. *Let the fat man sweat*, he thought. At last he said, "I've come through some bad times ... but I've survived. One day it'll get me. Maybe today ... maybe not!"

Skinny Chuck was on his feet. He ignored his fishing rod and spun round on his seat. "So you believe the stories?"

The skipper shrugged. "There are just so many," he sighed. "Look at the story of Flight 19! You know what happened to them!"

"No," Hank scowled. "Not exactly."

The skipper spread his hands. "It was 5 December 1945. Five Avenger planes set off on a training exercise from Fort Lauderdale. They were due to start by flying east. That would have taken them directly over our heads here ... in fact, they say that on calm days like today you can still hear the rumble of their engines!"

The fishermen strained their ears. There was only the soft lapping of the Atlantic against the boat – but they imagined the faint drone of aircraft engines and they shivered in the hot afternoon sun.

The old man leaned forward and spoke quickly. "The flight leader was Lieutenant Charles Taylor – an experienced man. Most of the other 13 pilots and gunners and radio operators were just students. Fourteen men – three to each plane!"

"Hang on! Hang on there!" Hank protested. "Three-fives is 15. Least, it was when I went to school."

The skipper nodded. "One man asked to be excused at the last moment. He said he had a strange feeling something was going to happen on the flight that day! Turns out he was right!"

"What happened?" Hank asked.

"The flight took off at 2:10 in the afternoon. It was perfect flying weather, with a light north-east wind and the planes were fuelled up to fly 1,000 miles. Around an hour later – at just about this time to be exact – Fort Lauderdale started to get messages from Lieutenant Taylor."

"Messages?" Chuck squeaked.

The skipper stood up and started to act out the scene in Taylor's plane. " 'This is Taylor calling base! Taylor calling base! This is an emergency! We seem to be off course. We cannot see land! Repeat! We cannot see land!' "

"Where were they?" Chuck squeaked.

"Just what the control tower asked! Taylor said, 'We are not sure of our position! We cannot be sure where we are! We seem to be lost!' The tower told him to head back to the west and that's when Taylor said the most amazing thing of all!"

"What was that?" Chuck asked, perched on the edge of his seat.

"He said, 'We don't know which is west! Everything is wrong – strange. We can't be sure of any direction – even the ocean doesn't look the way it should! Both my compasses have failed!'"

"That can't happen!" fat Hank sniffed.

The skipper took a small compass from his pocket. The fishermen didn't see the little magnet he held in the other hand. When they looked at the compass the needle was swinging wildly. Chuck gasped. "It's happening to us! I've heard this happens in the Devil's Triangle. How will we get back?"

"I'll just head towards the sun," the skipper said. "No problem."

"So why didn't they just do that?" Hank asked suspiciously.

"No use heading in any direction if you don't know where you are to start with! You could end up on the moon that way!" the skipper chuckled. "Anyway, the messages became fainter. Some interference was making the radio waves break up."

"Same thing that makes the compass go haywire," Chuck suggested.

"Could be, could be. Anyway, the tower at Fort Lauderdale heard odd messages that were being sent from plane to plane. The pilots were getting worried about running short of fuel. Lieutenant Taylor told his men that when the first plane ran out they would all land on the water together."

"They had life rafts?" Hank asked.

"They had," the skipper shrugged. "But they aren't much use if your plane cracks up when it hits the water and goes straight to the bottom!"

"Didn't they send out rescue planes?" Chuck wailed.

"They sent out a flying boat from Banana River Air Station – and what do you think happened to that?" The fishermen shook their heads. "That didn't return either! A tanker ship reported a burst of flames and a patch of oil – that would have been the rescue plane going down – but the next day they searched a quarter of a million square miles of ocean and not the slightest trace of Flight 19 was ever seen again."

Hank swallowed hard. "What do you think happened?" he croaked.

The skipper scratched his beard again. "If you ask me, I favour the UFO theory. Thirty years after the flight went down a reporter heard a story that Taylor's radio messages had been picked up at another radio station. Taylor had cried out, 'Don't come after me! They look like they are from outer space!' I guess aliens have some sort of watch on this area."

"You don't believe that?" the skinny fisherman laughed nervously.

"That's the only way to explain five aircraft vanishing into thin air. No wreckage, no trace. Yep. Aliens. Every now and then they snatch a ship or a plane and just zap it up to their space ship. It's always a one-way journey, though."

"We're not a plane – we can't crash," Hank argued. He tried to chuckle but the sound died in his throat.

"That's true!" the skipper agreed cheerfully. "Though the Devil's Triangle was claiming ships for hundreds of years before planes were even invented," he said.

"Oh," was all Chuck managed to say. He was turning as white as his baseball cap.

"Sure. The problem in the old days was the terrible calms you get here. Sailing ships hit this place called the Sargasso Sea and they just drifted to a standstill. By the time the winds picked up the crew had died of thirst or starvation. Many's the ship that's been discovered rotting in the Sargasso Sea with nothing but skeletons to welcome you. It's what they call the Horse Latitudes up here."

"Why's that?"

"Because Spanish treasure ships used to throw their horses overboard to try and save water."

Hank shuddered. He loved horses.

"Some ships just sailed into the triangle and never sailed out again," the skipper went on. "But the weirdest of all were the ships that were found completely deserted. Good ships where the crew had just disappeared into thin air. Sometimes they found a ship's cat or a dog on board. But one time they found that even the ship's parrot had vanished. You've heard of the famous *Mary Celeste*?"

"That's the ship that was found abandoned 100 years ago?" Chuck asked. "Was that in the Bermuda Triangle?"

"It was. Perfectly good ship. Found adrift with not a soul on board – living or dead."

"Of course, that was in the days before radio. But even after radio was invented there were strange messages coming from ships in the triangle. A Japanese freighter in 1924 sent a distress signal. It said, *Danger like a dagger now – come quickly – we cannot escape!* What sort of danger could that be, do you suppose? Eh? Something like nothing on Earth. That's what makes you think they may have been kidnapped by some aliens up there."

Chuck's scrawny neck was stretched like a chicken's as he squinted up towards the sky. "Can you get us out of here?" he moaned.

"You've paid for a day's fishing and you've caught nothing yet. Your friend says I don't get paid if you don't catch fish. I thought we could just hang around until you caught a few…"

"I'll pay you!" Hank spat. "Just get us out of here!"

"I'll pay an extra 50 bucks if you get us back in one piece!" Chuck wailed and wound in the fishing line as fast as his skinny hands could manage it.

"You're in charge," the skipper said. He turned and walked towards the cabin. He started the motor and glanced towards the large compass that pointed steadily north.

With his head bent over the control panel neither of the fishermen could see the great grin under the grey beard.

Solve the mystery

What happened to Flight 19? Can you explain how five aircraft lost their way then disappeared? Is there an area of the Atlantic Ocean where it's especially dangerous to enter? That's quite important to know if you ever sail or fly that way! It's a mystery … or is it?

Here are some facts that the storytellers forget to mention…

- Lieutenant Taylor was drunk the night before the flight and had a bad hangover. He tried to get out of flying that day. Taylor was the most experienced pilot on Flight 19 and he was not in a good state to fly. The rest of the crew were just trainees. No mystery, just human weakness.

- Taylor's compass broke soon after he took off – *not* while he was flying through the Devil's Triangle. He could still work out his position by looking at the sun. This method is called "dead reckoning" and it works well if you know the correct time. Taylor wasn't wearing a watch and kept asking his crew what time it was. No mystery, just human forgetfulness.

- Taylor soon became lost because he had no watch. Then he spotted an island he thought he recognized as one in the Bahamas. He was wrong. He set off to fly north and then east. He was flying out into the Atlantic Ocean when he thought he was flying towards his base. No mystery, just human error.

- The radios were not disturbed by strange forces but there was a faulty receiver at the base. And of course, the radio signals did become weaker as the planes flew further from their base. Taylor was told to switch to the emergency channel. That would probably have saved the flight. But one of his planes couldn't get that channel and it would be cut off – in the rain and darkness that plane could have lost touch. Taylor refused to switch to the emergency channel. No mystery, just human stubbornness.

- The weather wasn't calm. Flight 19 was heading into storms and rain. Once the sun disappeared behind the clouds he became even more confused. Several of the pilots told him to turn west but he ignored them. Because they had to follow orders they went with him out over the Atlantic. No mystery, just human discipline.

● When the planes ran out of fuel they'd try to land on the water and climb into life rafts. But the crew were young and had never been trained in emergency landings. In stormy weather, in the darkness, the Avenger planes would have sunk before the crews could escape. There were no life rafts because no one had time to get out. By the time the planes ran out of fuel they'd be over the deepest part of the Atlantic – 10,000 metres deep. The water is so deep that they would sink too far for them ever to be found. No mystery, just natural forces.

Other parts of the story are simple lies. Taylor did NOT call, "Even the ocean doesn't look the way it should!" That was invented years later.

It's true that the rescue aircraft disappeared too. But it blew up 23 seconds after take-off. Those Mariner seaplanes were known to have faulty fuel tanks and several of them had exploded in this way. No mystery – just a lit cigarette, probably.

So if Flight 19 wasn't a mystery, where did the idea of a Devil's triangle come from? Here is an explanation...

It started, just as in the story, with sailors telling stories. Just for fun they invented the legend to scare young sailors out there for the first time. "We're heading into the unknown, lad! People have passed into this part of the ocean and never been seen again!" Then, when the young sailor turned pale and started muttering prayers, the old sailors would have a good laugh.

In time people began to notice that ships did disappear in this part of the ocean – natural forces make it dangerous with strong currents and magnetic problems with reading a compass. When some unfortunate ship was lost then mysterious forces were blamed.

When the famous Mary Celeste *was found adrift with no crew aboard then the Devil's triangle was blamed – even though that ship was found nowhere near the triangle! One ship supposed to be "swallowed" by the Bermuda Triangle was in fact in the Indian Ocean at the time. And that's on the other side of the world!*

The sea has claimed victims all over the world – not just in the Bermuda Triangle. Some mysteries remain unexplained…

1. *The Hermania*. The disappearance of the crew of the *Mary Celeste* is remembered as a great sea mystery. But the ship's boat had gone and it is clear that they had tried to escape to safety. The only mystery is *why* they abandoned the ship. Much stranger was the ship *Hermania*, found drifting off the Cornish coast in 1849. The ship's masts had been blown away – and so had her crew. There was no sign of anyone and the ship's lifeboat was still on board. Had they all been swept away by a single wave? Or had they jumped into the water to swim ashore rather than take the lifeboat? Or were they abducted by aliens? We'll never know.

2. *The James B Chester*. An even stranger disappearance happened in the middle of the Atlantic Ocean in 1855. The ship *James B Chester* was found abandoned but, unlike the *Hermania*, it hadn't been battered by a storm. It was in good condition. The ship's papers and the compass were missing – a few possessions seemed to have been snatched from drawers. Like *Mary Celeste* it looked as if the crew had taken to the lifeboat for some unknown reason … except all the lifeboats were in place! It's a mystery.

3. *The Iron Mountain*. A ship sinking in a vast ocean can easily disappear for ever. Even a huge ship like the *Titanic* took 80 years to find. But a ship on a river should not vanish without trace. Yet that's what appears to have happened to the riverboat *Iron Mountain*. The 60-metre riverboat was towing barges full of cotton up the Mississippi. When it set sail in July 1872 it had more cargo on the deck and 52 passengers.

The barges were seen drifting downstream – the rope to the *Iron Mountain* appeared to have been cut. But no trace of the ship, its deck cargo or its 52 passengers were ever seen again. The Mississippi is a big river … but not big enough to swallow all that and leave no wreckage, surely?

4. The Mediterranean USO. Most people have heard of Unidentified Flying Objects (UFOs) but few have heard of Unidentified Submarine Objects (USOs) – that is, un-explained sightings at sea. In August 1962, for example, three fishermen were working in the Mediterranean near Marseilles. It was late at night and they saw what looked like a sub-marine moving over the surface of the water. They watched from about 300 metres away as frogmen started to climb aboard. The fishermen called through a megaphone but the frogmen ignored them. Only the last one on to the submarine turned and waved an arm. After he was inside, the craft rose above the water with red and green lights flashing. The lights went

out and the craft started to spin and glow orange. Suddenly it shot into the air and vanished in the direction of the stars. A lot of USOs were also seen near Italy in 1978 but no one got as close as those fishermen. What did they see? Were they telling the truth? Why would they lie? It's a mystery.

5. The sea crocodile. There have been stories of sea monsters for as long as there have been sailors. We probably know more about the moon than we do about the depths of the world's oceans. So some of the stories of monstrous creatures may just be true – and explain how humans can disappear from the decks of the ships, not kidnapped by aliens but eaten by monsters! In the First World War a German submarine captain hit a British ship with a torpedo as it crossed the Atlantic. The captain reported, "I watched the explosion. I saw the ship blown apart but I also saw a creature blown up into the air. It was 20 metres long and had a pointed snout and four limbs like paddles. The creature fell back into the sea and swam away." No one has seen such a sea crocodile before or since. What did the captain see? It's a mystery.

FACT • FILE •

WHO BURNED BORLEY?

Ghost hunter Harry Price became rich and famous by writing about a house, Borley Rectory. He called it "The most haunted house in England". When the house was destroyed Price wrote a follow-up book "The end of Borley Rectory" and made still more money. How much truth was there in the story? Price wasn't the only person to make money from its disastrous end...

Borley, England, February 1939

"Careful!" the man in the tweed suit cried. "The walls aren't safe! We wouldn't want you crushed under a falling wall, would we? You might not be insured!" Then he put back his head and laughed.

He stood in the empty doorway to a blackened ruin. The sharp smell of charred wood hung heavy in the air.

The man in the black suit clutched his briefcase to his thin chest and did not laugh. "Captain Gregson?" he asked.

"At your service." The man in the tweed suit smiled and gave a mock salute.

"I am Edward Thin from West Essex Insurance."

"Hah! Thin by name and thin by nature," Captain Gregson grinned.

Edward Thin did not grin. "I am here to investigate your claim for the destruction of your house by fire."

Gregson narrowed his eyes a little. "Investigate, is it? Well, here you are! It wasn't damaged in a flood or blown over by a gale. It caught fire and burned down. What else is there to investigate? Hah!"

Thin's mouth turned down at the corners. "The question of *how* the fire started," he said firmly. "Perhaps you can explain."

Gregson nodded. "I put it all down on the claim form, Mr Thin."

Thin coughed politely. "Exactly, Captain Gregson. That is why I have been sent to investigate. The manager at West Essex is a little concerned about parts of the claim."

"Hah! Doesn't believe in ghosts, does he?" Gregson asked. Before Thin could reply the man in tweed took him by the elbow and led him down the path to the gate that led out onto the quiet country road. "Come down to the Borley tavern. We'll have a bit of the landlord's excellent cheese and pickle and a jar of his best ale. Then I can tell you the story. Some of the locals are in there. They know the old stories even better than I do."

Before Thin could protest he found himself being led away from the grim, blackened shell of Borley Rectory and towards the low, stone inn on the village green. Gregson greeted everyone in the lounge bar with a cheery wave and ordered food and drink from the red-faced barman with the dreadful ginger wig. When he was sitting at a table with the insurance investigator he began his story. The rest of the people in the room sat back and listened.

"Borley's been called the most haunted house in England," Gregson began.

"And that's the truth," a woman at the next table cackled.

"It all began back in Tudor times before Henry VIII got rid of the monasteries. This was the site of a monastery."

"And a convent," the landlord in the red wig chipped in, placing a large wedge of cheese on the table. "That's how there was a nun there. She's the one that started it all!"

"That's right, George," Captain Gregson agreed. He bit into the cheese and kept talking, scattering crumbs over his black-suited guest. "The nun – a young French lass – fell in love with a monk. Of course, that was totally against the rules. They decided to run away together. One night she slipped out of the convent and met her lover in the lane. They went off on the London road."

"Didn't get very far," the woman at the next table put in. She smacked her toothless gums together. "They were caught and brought back. The abbess told them that if they wanted to be together they could stay together – for the rest of time! He was hanged while the French nun was put in a cavity in the wall and the abbess had it bricked up. Left her to die a horrible death, she did."

Captain Gregson tore off a chunk of bread and stuffed it in his mouth as he went on. "Of course, the nun had no Christian burial. That's why she has to for ever haunt the spot where she died."

Edward Thin picked at the cheese and said, "Perhaps you could simply tell me how the fire started, Captain Gregson."

"I'm coming to that, aren't I? My house that's just been burned was built just 100 years ago by the local vicar – the Reverend Henry Bull – for himself, his wife and 14 children. He built it on the site of the old convent. And that seemed to have disturbed the old nun's spirit."

"Henry Bull saw her walking across the lawn," the toothless woman put in. "So did the vicar's children. They walked over to her to ask what she was doing there and the nun vanished. Vanished into thin air!"

"Hah!" Captain Gregson chuckled. "That's what Mr Thin breathes! Thin air!"

The insurance man did not chuckle. "The fire, Captain Gregson."

"I'm coming to that. This Henry Bull died at the Rectory and then his son took over. The son died and *he* began to haunt the place too. When he was dying he'd promised he would! He was for ever throwing mothballs around the house."

"Tell him about the coach and horses," the landlord said.

"Ah, yes! They appear around midnight. They charge down the road outside the Rectory, turn in at the gate and vanish!" Captain Gregson said cheerfully. "We've all seen the coach – and the headless coach drivers too!"

Edward Thin blew out his cheeks impatiently, "Really, Captain Gregson, I don't see what this has to do with the fire!"

"He's coming to that!" the landlord put in. "It was after the next vicar moved in that the fun really began. He was the Reverend Smith and he invited the *Daily Mirror* in to investigate. Why, the village was packed with tourists for weeks! You couldn't move for ghost hunters!"

"But the one that did the most to make Borley famous was the ghost hunter Harry Price," the old woman went on. "Wrote a whole book about what he found there. He called Borley 'The most haunted house in England'."

"Why was that?" the insurance man asked even though he had tried hard not to show an interest.

"He found the house was full of them polly ghosts!" she told him.

"Poltergeists," an old man muttered.

"Aye, whatever. Ghosts that did more than just appear. They threw things around," she said.

"Things?"

"A glass candlestick, and slate and pebbles!" the landlord put in.

"And they talked to Harry Price! At least, the dead Reverend Bull did!" someone else reminded them.

"Aye!" the old woman crooned. " 'Are you the Reverend Bull?' he asked." The old woman gave three sharp raps on the table. *Rap! rap! rap!* "That was for yes. 'Are you happy?' " *Rap! rap!* "No! 'Do you mind the Reverend Smith living here?' "

Rap! rap! " 'Were you murdered?' " *Rap! Rap! Rap!*

"The Smiths moved out, of course," Captain Gregson sighed.

"And you moved in?" the insurance man asked, taking out a pen to make notes.

"No! That was eight years after they moved out, back in 1931. The next vicar was called Foyster. His wife had a terrible time with the ghosts. The nun started writing messages on the walls for her! 'Lights! Prayers! Help!' she wrote!"

"In French," the insurance man put in quietly.

"You what?"

"She was a French nun. Why didn't she write in French?" the investigator persisted.

For a moment Captain Gregson's mouth moved soundlessly then he said, "Why not go and ask her, old chap! She's probably still up there at the house."

"Is she prepared to appear in court?" the insurance man asked. It was his turn to smile. Captain Gregson did not smile.

"As I was saying … Marianne Foyster was the next woman to live there," he went on. "And she saw a hideous creature that struck her shoulder with a claw like iron. Her husband kept a whole diary of the throwings and the bells ringing and rapping noises and doors being locked and the things that were moved around. Horrible, Mr Thin."

"That didn't stop you buying the house," Thin said.

"No! No! I bought it as a deserted property. And then I heard about Harry Price's work. I contacted the chap – a truly great man and a marvellous spirit investigator. That's when he gave me the notes from one of his last ghost investigations." Gregson pushed a typed sheet across the table and let the insurance man study it.

Borley Séance

May 1938

Contact with spirit medium Sunex Amures

H. Price: Does anyone want to speak to us?

S. Amures: Yes.

H. Price: Who are you?

S. Amures: Sunex Amures. I am one of the men who plans to burn down Borley Rectory tonight at nine o'clock. This will be an end to the haunting. Go to the house and you will see us enter what belongs to us. In the ruins you will find the bones of the murdered spirit. This will be the proof you seek that the spirit died there.

H. Price: Is there a room where the fire will start?

S. Amures: In the hall. Yes, yes. You must go to the Rectory and find the proof.

Edward Thin sniffed. "The fire did not start that night. It started ten months later, didn't it Captain?"

"It did! Maybe the spirits have a different calendar to ours, eh?" Gregson chuckled.

"And it wasn't started by a spirit. It was started by you," the insurance man went on patiently.

"What? Good lord, no!"

"You were there at the time."

"I was ... I was in the hall. I was sorting out a stack of books. Then I felt a terrible chill wind blow in even though the door was closed! It was as if a huge hand was pushing the air down the hallway. It pushed the pile of books clean over. The books knocked over my paraffin lamp and it shattered. Of course, the paper caught fire and before I could move the hall was ablaze. I was lucky to escape with my life!"

"Some weren't so lucky!" the old woman wailed and gnashed her gums. "We all saw the fire and rushed up to the old house. We got there before the fire brigade! We looked up and saw a young woman at the upstairs window, didn't we?"

"There were no bodies found in the ruins when the police searched," Edward Thin said sharply.

"No!" the landlord told him. "That's because we saw two shadowy figures walk out through the flames in the doorway. The nun and her young love. Set free at last!"

The insurance man screwed the cap back on his pen and rose to his feet. "Good day, Captain Gregson," he said tartly.

"Well, Mr Thin? When can I expect to be paid my £7,000 for the house?" Captain Gregson asked, taking a deep sup of his ale.

The man in the black suit looked at him with eyes as cold as a haunted hall. "You are not insured against ghostly damage, Captain. I think you have more chance of being run over by a headless coachman than you have of getting paid by West Essex Insurance."

"I'm insured against *fire*!" Captain Gregson cried angrily. "Even if it's started by a *ghost*!"

"Yes, but you are *not* insured if it is started by *yourself*," Edward Thin said and the man in the black suit walked out of the tavern door as smoothly and silently as a phantom nun.

Solve the mystery

Who burned Borley? And was the place ever haunted?

Ghost hunters today still believe that the ghosts of Borley burned down their own home. These ghost hunters ignore what the insurance company said at the time in their report:

> *Captain W. E. Gregson claim for £7356 for the destruction by fire of his property, Borley Rectory on 27 February 1939.*
>
> *Our lawyer, Mr William Crocker, has advised us to reject this impudent claim for "accidental loss by fire". It is our opinion that Captain Gregson set fire to the place himself.*

Captain Gregson was never paid. He was probably a fraud and a liar. But he wasn't the first fraud and liar to visit Borley. Look at some of the ghost stories that surround the place...

- **The ghostly nun.** There was never a convent on the site of Borley Rectory. Even if a young French nun had lived nearby and run away with a monk then she would not have died that way. There was simply no such punishment for runaway nuns – ever.

- **The headless coachman.** This story was tagged on to the ghostly tales about Borley. But many villages in England have exactly the same legend. Once street lamps were introduced then the phantom coaches faded in their light.

- **The murdered vicar.** The Reverend Bull's spirit said he'd been murdered and blamed his wife. Bull's sisters hated his wife and they accused her of all sorts of wicked deeds. Those sisters were there when the "messages" were sent. The spirit messages said exactly what the sisters wanted to hear. The messages were probably faked to please the sisters who were paying for the séance.

- **The poltergeist.** Harry Price went to investigate the stories of rapping and throwing stones. Price was good at magic tricks and he did stone throwing and rapping so he got a good story. One reporter caught Price with a pocket full of stones but didn't publish the story of Price's cheating.

- **The mystic writing.** Marianne Foyster claimed that the messages on her wall were from a ghostly spirit. "Marianne. Please help." But if you study the ghost's handwriting you will see it is exactly the same as Marianne's handwriting! A mystery? No. Marianne wrote the messages herself. She was as great a fraud as Harry Price.

- **The séance messages.** The spirits of Borley gave messages which turned out to be true. Sunex Amures said that if the investigators dug in the ruins they would find a skeleton. And they did! A mystery? Not really. The skeleton was probably put there by Harry Price. He then said, "Let's dig where the spirit told us!" ... and he found the skeleton he'd planted a few weeks before.

Sunex Amures also said the house would burn down ... and it did! (Only ten months late.) Here is an explanation...

Captain W E Gregson had retired from the army. He had a small pension but it wasn't much to live on. The only house he could afford to live in was the half-ruined Borley Rectory. The last vicar, Foyster, had only lived in a few rooms of the vast, ugly house, and the rest were rotting and rat-infested. The house had no electricity fitted and not even any running water. Gregson got the house very cheap.

Gregson knew the local stories about the ghosts and got in touch with Harry Price. He told Price a few lies about ghostly experiences. Price told Gregson the Sunex Amures fire threat. Gregson had an idea.

Gregson insured the house for over £7,000. Three months later he took a pile of books into the hall and soaked them in paraffin. He then set light to the books and stepped out of the front door. Once he was sure the house was well ablaze he strolled slowly down to the village and called the fire brigade … who were far too late to save it.

Gregson hoped to get away with the fraud by blaming the ghosts. Ghost hunters then (and now) believed him. The sensible insurance people didn't.

Fakes and frauds – FACT FILE

In the world of mystery there have been many fakes. People tell tales for money, they tell them to get publicity and they tell them to scare their friends…

1. The ship-builder's ghost. Sunderland, in north-east England, was once the world's largest ship-building town. Many men died building the ships so it's not surprising there were ghost stories surrounding the shipyards. On the north bank of the River Wear there was a quay at Palmers Hill and the ghost there was supposed to be an old man pushing a creaking barrow. The ghostly figure had string around the bottom of his trousers – an old ship-builders' trick to stop the rats running up their trouser legs! One nervous young worker was sent to fetch tools, late at night. When he saw something that looked just like the ghost in the stories he fled back to his mates screaming in terror. Some years later an older worker admitted it was all a joke. He had hidden behind a shed and flapped a large piece of cardboard to make an eerie sound.

2. The Cottingley fairies. Some spirit jokes are taken really seriously and believed. In 1917 two Yorkshire girls, Frances and Elsie cut pictures of fairies from an old book. They then took pictures of themselves with the paper fairies and said they were real. It was a joke, but Sir Arthur Conan Doyle said they were real. Conan Doyle was the writer of the Sherlock Holmes mystery stories and if he said something was true then people believed it. The first of the pictures shows four fairies flying in front of Frances who sits in front of a waterfall. The waterfall was moving and the camera was slow so the water is blurred. But the fairies are supposed to be flying … why weren't they blurred? No one thought to ask! Elsie's dad asked, "How could a brilliant man like Conan Doyle believe in such a thing?" That's the real mystery. The answer is, "You can believe in anything if you *want* to." And Doyle wanted to believe in spirits.

3. The haunted wardrobe. In Berkshire, England, in 1937 a woman advertised a wardrobe for sale complete with a ghost. She was flooded with answers. People desperate for the wardrobe offered her up to £50 for it – a fortune for a piece of second-hand furniture in those days. The seller told tales of a little man who appeared through the door and of strange sounds coming from inside. In the end it was sold to a couple who owned a hotel. They

FACT • FILE

found they had lots of guests paying extra to sleep in the room with the haunted wardrobe. The ghost never appeared. Was it disturbed by the move? A mystery? Probably not. The ghost story was just a good way to make money. If you advertised a plain wardrobe for sale you'd get two or three people willing to pay two or three pounds. Advertise a *haunted* wardrobe and you'll get hundreds of people falling over themselves to pay ten times what it's worth!

4. The phantom UFO. Late in 1993 the South Yorkshire Police sent a message round to all of their patrol cars. "A flying saucer has landed in Kearsley Lane, Doncaster." Several people turned up to see this incredible sight. They were all arrested. The police were annoyed at people who bought radio receivers and listened to police messages; tuning to police wavelengths is against the law. The people who turned up to see the UFO had obviously broken the law.

5. The fortune teller. People who can see into the future give us one of the greatest mysteries. Ursula "Mother" Shipton lived in northern England in the early 1500s and looked into the future. Her predictions have been published many times over the years and many people claim they are miracles. In 1935, for example, the old king was dying and the next king was going to give up his throne so three kings would reign in one year. Followers of Mother Shipton printed her amazing prophecy, written 400 years before...

> *In nineteen hundred and thirty-five*
> *Which of us shall be alive?*
> *Many a king shall end his reign.*

Amazing? How did she know? A mystery?

Not really. The followers were so keen to show Mother's power they cheated. What the old witch actually wrote for the first line was:

> *In eighteen hundred and thirty-five...*

A big difference and no miracle.

DID THE WAXWORK MOVE?

Some of the world's greatest mysteries are the ones where the "impossible" seems to happen. One of the most ancient mysteries is the link between the body and the spirit. When the spirit leaves the body can the body still move? The ancient Egyptians believed it could. That's why they preserved the bodies of their kings as mummies – so the spirit could still walk and talk again in the afterlife. Can a dummy model of a person be filled by a spirit and live again? Some stories suggest that they can…

1857, Sacramento, USA

Sit down. I know why you're here. You've come to hear the story of the waxwork, haven't you?

I've told hundreds of stories to the newspapers but the waxwork story is the one they all want to hear. You must be the tenth young reporter who's come knocking at my door. I'll tell you the same as I told them. The truth, the whole truth and nothing but the truth.

It will cost you money. After all, it's a good story and one day I may want to turn it into a book. Let's say ten dollars, shall we? My story has to be worth ten dollars after all I went through.

All right, five dollars. Pay me now, then I'll start my story. Thanks.

Let's see. Where did it begin? It began in a bar room in Sacramento. I was sitting at the window looking across the street at the carnival that had come into town.

There was all the usual stuff – freak shows with bearded ladies and living skeletons, boxing champs who offered to fight anybody for a dollar. There were even some roundabout rides powered by a steam engine.

I wasn't very interested, I have to tell you. There are robberies and there are people tricked out of their money. The sheriff has a tough time with drunks when the carnival comes to town, but that's nothing special for me to report.

That night the bar room had gone quiet. A few lanterns threw light over the dusty road but even the carnival lamps were going out and most of the street was in shadow.

Anyway, there I was sitting at the window when I saw a tall man in a black suit and hat crossing the road. He had his arm round an old guy with grey whiskers and a buckskin suit. The old guy looked as if he was dying.

People stopped and stared, the way they do, but no one went to help. I saw the man in black was helping the old guy across to the saloon so I jumped to my feet and opened the door for him. "Thank you, sir," the man in black said.

"Can I help?"

"You could get old Josh here a drink, sir," the man in the black suit said.

I went to the bar and bought the old guy a double shot of whiskey and carried it across to the table. The tall man helped the old man to sip it. It burned his throat and he coughed a little but he held it down. "Thanks, stranger!" old Josh croaked.

"You taken ill?" I asked.

The two men looked at one another. "No, not exactly," the old man said carefully. That was when I got the scent of a story in my nose.

"So what happened? You been robbed?" I asked.

Old Josh shook his head. "No. But I've been scared half way to death. In fact, I may not live to see tomorrow. I sure as hell won't ever sleep again!"

"Tell me about it," I urged. He shook his head. I walked back to the bar and brought back whiskey for the three of us.

The man in black said, "Allow me to introduce myself, sir. I am Nathaniel Turner, proud owner of Turner's Wonderful Waxwork Museum." He stretched out a thin hand. I noticed the cuff of his jacket was frayed and stained with ink to hide the worn edge. I did the same thing myself to save on clothes. Mr Turner's waxworks were not doing good business I guessed.

I grasped his hand. "I'm Luke Gretz, reporter for the *Sacramento Star* newspaper."

Turner looked amused. "A *star* reporter, eh?"

I clicked my tongue. "Not so much of a star," I told him. "If I don't come up with the stories I'll be on the next stage back to Red Bluff stoking boilers on the paddle steamers!"

Turner took a deep breath, glanced at old Josh and said, "I think, sir, we may be able to help you there. We have a story so remarkable it would sell newspapers from Sacramento to Switzerland! A story so incredible it could make you a star in the very heavens itself! A story so important that when it's made you famous newspapers will kneel down and beg you to work for them!"

Nathaniel Turner was a showman. A good talker. I asked him bluntly, "What's in it for you?"

He spread his hands innocently. "A small increase in visitors to my humble waxworks, perhaps," he suggested.

"I write the story and you get free advertising," I nodded. "So give me the story."

"It's Josh's story really," he said. "But I can start it for him, if I may, sir. Two years ago I went across to London, England to visit. And I saw an exhibition by a woman called Madame Marie Tussaud. This Madame Tussaud had been around in the days of the French Revolution. She had the job of taking the heads of the dead nobles and making casts of their faces. She then turned these into wax models."

"I've heard of it," I told him.

"She toured her exhibition round England and then set up in Baker Street. That's where I saw the show and decided to bring it to America."

"Old Madame was dead but her son showed me around behind the scenes. He even offered to let me have one of the heads to bring back. It would be the start of my own collection to tour with the carnival."

"That was generous of him," I said.

Josh gave a sudden laugh. "You get nothing for nothing in this life, mister. It was like giving somebody a rattlesnake as a present!"

Turner nodded. "It seems the model I took had a … history. It was the head of a man called Nicodeme Leopold-Lepide. This Leopold-Lepide had been a tax collector in the days before the Revolution. He was ruthless and cruel. Anyone who failed to pay had their house and land taken from them. Their whole family was thrown on the streets to starve. They say, sir, he had a stone where other men have a heart!"

"Nice guy," I muttered.

"When Leopold-Lepide was executed there were thousands turned up to cheer his death. They led him to the guillotine and they say he had a faint smile on his cruel face. It was almost as if he knew this wasn't the end for him. Still, his head was sliced off and Madame Tussaud was waiting to take the head and make a waxwork out of it. The skin was tinted to look alive and the glass eyes were exactly the right shade of blue, they say. But after a few weeks they stopped putting the dummy of Leopold-Lepide on display."

"Why?" I asked.

"They never told me, sir. And I never guessed … until last week. I found that the dummy of old Leopold-Lepide wasn't all it seemed."

Old Josh supped at his whiskey and smacked his lips noisily. "You see, mister, we'd built a copy of the guillotine – not a working one, of course!" he cackled. "But in the dim light the red paint on the blade looked like blood. We stood old Leopold-Lepide beside it, waiting to be executed and that faint little smile gave everyone the creeps."

"Great," I said. "So what?"

"So, mister, one morning I opened up and went to dust off

the waxworks and sweep the passageways," Josh went on. "When I got to the Revolution scene I saw Leopold-Lepide's head on the floor. Its blue eyes just stared up at me and the smile was still on its lips. At first I thought some late visitor had knocked it off!"

"I fixed it back on," the owner explained. "Then we checked it before we locked up for the night. The head was as secure as yours, Mr Gretz, sir! But next morning, there it was on the floor."

"Someone was getting in," I said. "Some joker."

"My thoughts exactly!" Turner cried. "I said to Josh here that we'd set a trap. Spend a night in the museum and catch this joker."

"And you did?" I asked. The story was starting to grip me and I could see it gripping the *Sacramento Star* readers.

"I dusted that figure every day and it never moved," the old man said. "It couldn't hurt me, could it?"

"I don't know. Could it?" I asked.

"I guess it was around midnight when I heard a noise," Josh breathed. "Could have been mice – could have been someone picking at the door lock. I turned the lamp up just a shade. For some reason there was just one thing that caught my attention – Leopold-Lepide's eyes were staring at me. I mean straight at me! And that wasn't a wax skin. It was too … too real! The arm moved first. Slowly, but it was moving. Then the legs. The creature turned to face us. Then the face moved … that was the worst of all. It was frowning!"

Turner took up the story. "Last of all the lips moved. And it spoke. True as I'm sitting here, sir, that waxwork spoke to us. Now I've been to Paris, France and I speak a bit of their lingo. Leopold–Lepide was saying, 'Can I not get *any* peace? Not even at night? The French people came in their hundreds to see me executed. Now you come to see my spirit trapped in wax. Stay away … or you'll be sorry!'"

"What did you do?" I asked. I had my notebook in my pocket but I knew those words would stay burned in my brain.

"What did we do, mister?" Josh choked. "We got the heck out of it, sir! And the hounds of Hell wouldn't get me back in there at night again! Mr Turner had to practically carry me over here! I'm not sure yet if I'll ever get over it!"

I looked at the two men. They seemed truly shaken by what they'd seen. It was a good story … but I knew there was a better one waiting to be written. "Would you let me spend a night in the museum?" I asked.

"You are ready to risk your life for a story, sir?" Turner asked.

"I am."

He stroked his long chin. "It'll cost you $25," he said.

I rose to my feet. "I'll talk to my editor," I promised. "I'll be back around closing time tomorrow night."

"With the money, sir?" Turner asked quickly.

"With the money."

He rose to his feet. "We'll be ready for you," he promised.

I had no problem talking the editor into the stunt. At $25

it was cheap. And I wasn't too worried about what would happen. All I wanted was a feel for the place. I wanted some real atmosphere.

I got more than I expected, though, didn't I? Hell, you've read the article I wrote. Here it is. I won't tell you again how it happened. Read it for yourself...

SACRAMENTO ★ STAR

As I sat in the gloom of the lantern, the dim flickering light fell on the rows which were so strangely like human beings. Their stillness made them seem even more strange and ghastly. I listened for the sound of their breathing and the rustle of their clothes.

For an hour or two I sat facing these figures and felt brave enough. I mean, they were only waxworks...

And waxworks don't move. But every time I looked away from the tax collector then looked back he seemed to be in a slightly different pose.

I kept looking until I saw something. The waxwork's arm did move. Slowly at first, then faster it raised its two hands. Suddenly it snapped off its head! I stared, terrified, gripping the chair. Then, to make it worse, the wax head was replaced by a ghostly face. And that face had the cruellest, most evil sneer you ever saw.

It moved down from its stand. I jumped to my feet and stood to face it. The most frightening thing was that I could see clean through its head!

I backed into the door. I tapped on it. I wanted Josh Potter to see this for himself. But there was no answer! He was asleep! I banged harder while the ghost came closer. I turned my back on it and hammered on the door. I screamed when I felt those greasy wax hands on my neck. I screamed again … then I think I fainted. The next I knew I woke up in Josh Potter's arms.

I swear by all that's holy that this story is true.

So there you have it. The true story of the living waxwork. Mr Turner and me – we found the head lying on the floor beside the guillotine. The body was beside the door.

And the wax fingers were flat on the ends … as if they'd squeezed something hard. Turner went on to make a small fortune from that show. No one ever saw the figure move again, but that once was enough for me.

The editor was pleased enough with my work. I could have become that star reporter, I guess. But for some reason I just lost my nerve. My hand is too shaky to write a word these days. And I don't sleep too good.

That's why they gave me this job. Stoking the boilers on this riverboat. It's dark down here but it's hot as Hell. If that wax dummy ever tries to come after me I guess he'll melt clean away.

Now, if you'll excuse me, I've just got to stoke up this fire.

Solve the mystery

The waxwork story caused a sensation in all the American newspapers of the time. The most amazing, of course, was the article above, written by a man who had seen the waxwork moving for himself.

There are many possible explanations for this strange story. Here are just five. Which one do you prefer ... or can you think of a better one?

- **The ghost.** Leopold-Lepide was so evil his spirit was rejected by heaven. His ghost was doomed to walk the earth as a punishment. He haunted the waxworks where Madame Tussaud's image of his living face was on show. The waxwork didn't move ... what people saw was the ghost of Leopold-Lepide.

- **The mummy.** There is a true story about an exhibit at a Californian Amusement Park. For 50 years the *Horror House* showed a mysterious figure and claimed it was a mummified body. It chilled people for years and they happily paid to see it ... but in their hearts they didn't really believe there was a corpse underneath the bandages. They knew it was a dummy, not a mummy. In December 1976 a television company decided to film in the *Horror House* – they were making an episode of a popular serial called *The Six Million Dollar Man*. In the crowded little room a cameraman bumped into the mummy and its arm fell off … to reveal human bones and dried flesh underneath!

The corpse was rushed to a doctor. Police suspected it was a murder victim who'd been cunningly hidden in the *Horror House*! The doctor confirmed that the man had died of a bullet wound … but he'd been dead for 80 years or so. Perhaps Leopold-Lepide haunted his own body.

● **The nightmare.** The owner, the caretaker and the reporter were frightened men. They believed that the waxwork was possessed by an evil spirit. They didn't really see it move, but they were so terrified they *imagined* that it moved. They suffered from a *hallucination* – a sort of waking nightmare. The waxwork was really harmless, but a weak joint kept making the head drop off.

● **The joker.** Someone was playing a practical joke on Turner, Potter and the reporter. They knew of a secret entrance to the museum and were able to sneak in each night and knock the head off the tax collector model. When Turner and Potter spent the night in the museum they saw the joker moving around. They were so terrified they didn't wait to see exactly what (or who) was moving about in the shadows. They panicked and ran. The newspaper reporter made the same mistake.

● **The trick.** A reporter asked if he could spend a night in the museum because that would make a good story.

Nathaniel Turner decided to give him a great story. He hired some actor to dress up as the waxwork and the actor took the place of the dummy just before the reporter was locked in the room. He "came to life" after a couple of hours and scared the reporter half to death.

But is there another explanation…?

Nathaniel Turner wanted to make money. Lots of money. His waxwork show was rather dull and boring. So he made up a story about a living, moving waxwork to bring in curious customers. The caretaker, Josh Potter, swore the story was true because he was well paid by Nathaniel Turner to tell that story. The newspaper reporter went along with the lies; it made a good story and he'd sell more papers.

All three men, the owner, the caretaker and the reporter, were in on the trick. The waxwork never moved.

Do people come back to earth after death? It's a mystery but some stories seem to prove that they do…

1. The phantom sailor. Two young sailors were saved from a sinking ship by a ghostly man in a lifeboat. He kept saying "Two lives saved make up for two lives lost." He also told them to take a message to his wife – he gave his name, his address in Scotland and the hiding place of his money hoard. The rescuer vanished promising to send help. The sailors were rescued. One of them found the wife at the given address; the money was exactly where the rescuer had said it would be. But the wife also said her husband had died eight years before. He'd become drunk and jumped overboard – two crew members who went to his rescue died. Is that what the ghost meant, "Two lives saved make up for two lives lost."? Do guilty ghosts stay on this earth till they have paid for their sins?

2. The avenging ghost. Lord Inverawe was a British soldier fighting against native American Indians in 1758. He was told that the fort they were about to attack was called Ticonderoga. "Then I will die tomorrow," he said. Many years before he had sheltered his cousin's killer. His cousin's ghost demanded that Lord Inverawe should murder the killer. Lord Inverawe refused. "Then beware Ticonderoga! You will die there!" the ghost warned. Lord Inverawe asked every traveller he met but no one could tell him where Ticonderoga was … until he arrived there with his troop of soldiers. Just as the ghost predicted, Lord Inverawe died. Do murder victims stay on earth till they have been avenged?

3. The unhappy ghost. The Tower of London has been the scene of many horrific deaths and executions. It is said to be haunted by the ghosts of some of the people who have died there. The most famous ghost is that of Henry VIII's wife, Anne Boleyn, who was beheaded at the Tower and has been seen walking around with her head tucked under her arm. His fifth wife, Catherine Howard, heard that she was also going to be executed and ran screaming to Henry at Hampton Court palace. Her screaming ghost can be seen there, it is said. Do spirits return to haunt the place where they suffered terrible misery?

4. The goodbye ghost. A woman called Mrs Paquet went into the kitchen in her Chicago flat. There she saw the image of her brother. She knew her brother was working on a tug-boat in

FACT·FILE

the harbour. A ghostly rope seemed to wrap around his legs and he tumbled backwards. "My brother is drowned!" she cried. Sure enough, at that very moment her brother was thrown into the river when a stray rope whipped around his legs. There are many reports of people seeing relatives – often when they were oceans apart – at the moment they die. Do spirits visit their loved ones as they are about to leave this world?

5. The friendly ghost. The Earl of Strafford was the chief adviser to King Charles I ... and he went on advising him over four years after he died! Strafford was executed in 1641. King Charles then went to war with the forces of Parliament and met them at Naseby near Leicester. The night before the battle Strafford's ghost appeared to Charles and several other people warning them to avoid a battle on the next day. Charles ignored the ghost and lost the battle. A few years later the king also lost his head on the scaffold. Do ghosts return to earth to warn their friends of disasters?

WHAT DID THE DRIVER SEE?

There are some mystery stories that are passed on from one person to another and they start with the words, "This is a true story that happened to a friend of a friend of mine…" Of course, you can never find out where the stories started and they are usually just made up. But occasionally one of these stories comes along where the facts are on record. Police record…

Kent, southeast England, 1992

It was one of those quiet nights when you think nothing will happen. That's exactly the time when something unexpected can always catch you out.

The A229 road towards Maidstone was quiet. It was just gone midnight and most of that corner of England was asleep in bed. The moon glimmered on the road and it stretched out like a silver ribbon in front of Ian Sharpe.

Ian yawned and stretched and settled back in the seat of his car. He pressed the accelerator gently and sped past the limit. But the tyres were new, the brakes effective and the road empty. It was perfectly safe.

Ian chuckled to himself. "No law against doing 85 miles an hour … just a law against getting caught!" The road was straight and clear and he didn't expect to see any police cars.

The car raced under the bridge and past Blue Bell Hill. When he saw the turning to Aylsford he knew he'd just four miles to go to home. He'd be in bed in ten minutes.

He was dreaming of slipping beneath the electric blanket when it happened. One moment the road was empty. The next a pale shape was there at the side of the road. His foot covered the brake as the shape rushed closer.

It was a girl. A fair-haired girl in a light blouse and dress. He began to brake gently.

What was she doing alone by the side of a main road? Perhaps she needed help. He'd pull up and ask her if she was OK. But as he drew closer she suddenly stepped out into the path of his car.

His headlights picked out her face. A pretty face but with no expression and no fear as his car skidded towards her. Ian cried out as he careered into her and she disappeared under the front of his car.

He must have skidded on for another 20 metres before the car shuddered to a stop. It took him a few seconds to gather his breath and swallow the sickness that was rising in his throat. His hands were numb as he fumbled for the door handle and tugged it open. The sharp tang of smoking rubber stung his nostrils. "I couldn't have stopped any quicker," he murmured to himself.

The cold night air rushed into the car and revived him like a bucket of water in the face. He stepped out of the car and looked back up the dark road, lit only by the tail-lamps of his car. The road was empty.

He knew that there was only one place the girl could be. She must be trapped and crushed under his car. He couldn't drive off to the nearest phone for help while she was there. He couldn't run off and leave her. All he could think of was jacking up the car and pulling her out. He could drive her into Maidstone Hospital if she was still alive.

But first he had the sickening task of looking under the car and seeing just how badly damaged she was. "I couldn't help it!" he moaned. He sniffed back tears and dropped to his knees. He lowered his head and looked under the car.

There was no one there.

He took a huge breath and rubbed his tired eyes. "She must have been knocked into a ditch," he said. He snapped on the car warning lights. They flashed orange as he began to walk back up the road, peering into the deep grass at the edge of the road.

As he reached the start of his black tyre marks they were lit by the headlamps of a car heading in the same direction. It would see the warning lights flash and slow down. The driver could turn his headlamps on to the grass verge and help him find the girl in the pale clothes easily.

Sure enough the car slowed as it approached. Ian stepped out into the roadway and waved a hand. He was dazzled by the headlamps and couldn't see the driver's face for the glare but he heard the car crash down a gear, the engine roar and the wheels spin as the newcomers raced off towards Maidstone.

Ian swore at the driver and waved his arms helplessly. The next car was coming from Maidstone and that too slowed, then raced away. No one wanted to stop on a lonely road to help a stranger.

Ian walked slowly back to his car, his knees weak and

shaking. He checked once more to see that there was no girl under his car, then he climbed in and started the engine. He drove off slowly and took ten minutes to reach Maidstone police station.

Sergeant Beckett was behind the desk, supping a cup of tea. He looked up as Ian Sharpe stood at the counter. "Sir? How can I help you?" He saw a tall, thin young man with a face as pale as dough and a haunted expression. "Are you all right, sir?"

"I think I've just killed somebody ... run her over in my car."

The sergeant walked around the counter and led Ian to a bench seat by the door. "Tell me about it."

Ian began – unsure at first but soon the story was pouring out. "I need help," he finished, "help to go and find her."

The policeman had been sitting close to Ian, his nostrils wide as if he was sniffing the air. "You haven't been drinking, sir?"

For the first time since he left the scene of the accident the young driver showed a flash of anger. "Certainly not! I've been to a business meeting in London. Can't we just get out to Blue Bell Hill as soon as possible?"

The policeman nodded. "I'll send a squad car out there now, get someone to cover me on the desk and I'll drive you back so you can show me exactly where this happened."

The police car had arrived first, its blue light flashing close to the place where Ian had skidded. The police driver was shining his torch on the road. "This where it happened?" Sergeant Beckett asked.

Ian looked at him, dazed. "How did you know?"

The policeman shook his head. "Let's just leave our lads to search. We'll go back to the station and you can have a hot cup of tea. You look like you've seen a ghost, lad."

They drove back to the station and parked at the front. Sergeant Beckett stepped out and walked slowly round the front of Ian's car. "It's surprising how much damage a human body can do to a car – even hitting a dog can wreck your radiator."

"What?" Ian Sharpe asked, still dazed.

"How fast were you going?"

Ian's pale face showed a pink spot in each cheek. "Sixty – maybe a little more."

"If you hit a girl at 60 then that bumper bar of yours would be dented, the radiator grille wrecked and there'd probably be damage to the bonnet too. I'd stake my sergeant's stripes that this car hasn't hit anybody tonight."

"But … but I don't see how I could have missed her! Do you think she could have thrown herself out of the way at the last second? Then run off before I could get out of the car?"

"Either that or you didn't see her at all," Sergeant Beckett said carefully. He led the way into the police station and sat on the cold, hard bench seat again. He ordered a young constable to bring them each a cup of tea and as they held the white plastic cups the policeman explained. "I was just a young PC 20 years ago when I first heard about a case like this. I wasn't on duty at the time but the station was full of it. The story of a strange accident at that very spot."

"Someone was killed?"

"Not exactly. No. Back in July 1974 a bricklayer called Maurice Goodenough was driving along that stretch when he believed he knocked over a girl. He got out of the car and found her lying on the road. He wrapped her in a blanket but decided it was best not to move her. He decided it would be best to come straight here to the station. We went back to the scene. And we found the blanket."

Ian sipped the tea and then looked at the sergeant. "But no girl?"

"But no girl. We searched the area thoroughly but we never found a trace."

"Who was she then? A ghost?" Ian breathed.

The sergeant shrugged. "If she was, then the most likely person was a young lady called Judith Rochester. She had been trying on some bridesmaid dresses – her friend was getting married the next day. They set off to meet the bridegroom at a local pub but they never made it. Their Ford

Cortina collided head on with a Jaguar at Blue Bell Hill."

"She died on the spot?"

"Not quite. She died in hospital the next day. Two other girls died within days and one survived – but she's never been able to remember anything about the accident. There are some as say it's Judith Rochester that haunts the road around the time of the year when it happened – November."

"And you?"

The police sergeant supped his tea and said, "Me? I don't believe in ghosts."

"So what did I see?"

"I don't know, sir. I wasn't there. I guess we'll just have to leave the file open. We'll put it down as a bit of a mystery, shall we sir?"

Solve the mystery

This story could be treated as a joke, as most "friend of a friend" stories are. But a curious thing happened two weeks after Ian Sharpe's encounter with the phantom crash victim.

19-year-old Christopher Dawkins was driving through the area when a young woman appeared to dash in front of his car. Yet again there was no damage to the car and no body to be found.

The most famous "friend of a friend" story is probably that of the phantom hitchhiker, in which a motorist stops to give a stranger a lift. When the motorist stops they then find the hitchhiker has vanished. The motorist later finds out that the phantom was identical to a person who died on the spot many years before.

The Sharpe and Dawkins story is similar to the phantom hitchhiker story in several ways:

● The phantom is usually that of a young girl.
● The phantom is almost always dressed in pale clothing.
● The incidents usually happen at night.
● The driver is always alone at the time of the incident.
● There is never anyone else who saw the same phantom at the same time.
● The phantom is usually seen on the same date as the victim died.

Sharpe saw the victim 11 days before the day of the girl's death and Dawkins saw her three days after the date. This particular phantom was determined to be killed again and again.

Is there an explanation – apart from the theory that the two drivers were lying? It is possible that they were *mistaken*. Here is an explanation...

Driving a car, late at night is tiring. Drivers can fall asleep with their eyes open. They are able to keep their car on the road though they are "dreaming" at the same time. Their brains know that this is dangerous and they desperately send a message to the dreamer saying "Wake up or you'll kill someone!" The most shocking "message" they can send is "If you're not careful you'll run over an innocent pedestrian!"

The dreamer sleeps on but the car headlights flash onto a road sign – a pale shape looming at the side of the road.

The dreaming driver wakes up and remembers that pale flicker of light – they are quite sure they've hit the pedestrian their waking brain was trying to warn them about.

This condition is given the name "highway hypnosis". Sharpe and Dawkins suffered the same effect at the same spot – perhaps a particular road sign lights up in a curious way as a car approaches. They both seriously believed they'd killed a girl.

FACT·FILE

There are many, many "friend-of-a-friend" tales going around. Some may have a little truth in them. Others are simply invented. Here are a few. Make up your own mind...

1. Iran. In 1956 Tony Clark was working in Iran and had to travel 120 miles to Tehran. He'd passed nowhere to stop and eat and he was starving so he was delighted when he eventually saw a sort of roadside café. He went in and enjoyed a meal that was cheap and delicious. The owner said he was delighted to have helped a stranger and invited Clark to return any time he liked and tell his friends about the café. But, when Clark did return to the exact spot three months later, there was no sign that a restaurant had ever existed there.

2. USA. A woman was driving home alone one night when she was scared by a man driving behind her. The man kept flashing his headlights at the woman. She refused to stop, hurried home and climbed out of the car. As she reached her front door the back door of her car opened and a strange man tumbled out and ran away. The car that had been following her pulled up and the driver explained. He had been following the woman when he saw a man with a knife rise up from the back seat. Flashing his lights had stopped the knifeman from killing the woman.

3. Britain. A man's car broke down in the streets of Sheffield. He raised the bonnet and looked for the fault. A car with three young men in pulled up and offered to tow him to the nearest garage. He agreed. But it happened that the three young men were car thieves who'd just stolen the car they were in. They set off towing the poor man through the streets at speeds up to 80 m.p.h. By the time the tow rope snapped and the car rolled to a halt the driver was shivering with terror.

4. France. In 1988 Didier Chassegrande, the driver of a 38-ton lorry, said that he had accidentally run over an old cyclist. He dragged the mangled body to the side of the road then went to find the nearest telephone. When the police arrived they found no bicycle and no corpse. All there was at the scene was a torch, a bicycle pump … and a set of false teeth!

5. Germany. The hitchhiker who disappears is a common "friend-of-a-friend" story. But a 1983 tale from Bavaria is a little unusual. The woman stopped to give a lift to a stranger with a straggling beard, a robe and sandals. He fastened his seat belt and they set off. He announced, "You should know that I am the Archangel Gabriel. I have come to tell you that the world is going to end on 31 October next year!" She fixed her gaze on the road while she overtook a truck. When she looked back at her passenger the seat was empty although the seat belt was still fastened … but the world didn't end in 1984, as you may have noticed!

? FACT • FILE •?

HOW DID THE YOUNG PRINCE DIE?

Some mysteries cause fierce arguments that go on for hundreds of years. In the year 1483 Prince Edward was due to be crowned King of England – he never made it. His Uncle Richard took the throne instead. And who was to blame for the fact that Prince Edward (and his little brother) were never seen in public again ... alive or dead? Not a difficult question! In Spain 80 years later, Prince Don Carlos died in his prison. But it wasn't a wicked uncle who was suspected – it was his own father...

July 1568, Convent Church of El Real, Madrid, Spain

"Who are we putting in this grave, Pappa?" the boy asked, looking down into the hole in the church's stone floor.

The gravedigger wiped sweat and golden dust off his brow. He took a long drink from the goatskin bottle and said, "The prince Don Carlos. Now shut up and keep working, Juan."

The boy took his small shovel and tidied the dusty earth that his father was throwing out of the hole. It was dim in the cathedral and that sheltered them from the worst of the summer heat. Still his father was hot and cross.

The clatter and scraping of the shovels echoed round the high walls. Painted plaster saints looked down on them. Nuns moved silently through the church, squinted at the new grave from the corners of fearful eyes and went on with their prayers.

Juan was glad when a cheerful, slightly chubby woman shuffled down the aisle towards them. "Mother!" Juan cried and was horrified to hear his voice echo from every corner. The nuns turned and glared at the boy.

The woman smiled and placed a finger against her lips. She unwrapped a cloth and showed the boy olives and a little ham and a fresh loaf of bread. "Dinner, Manuel," she said quietly to her husband. The gravedigger pulled himself up to the edge of the grave where he sat, his feet dangling into the hole. His wife and son sat at each side of him.

Juan was glad of the chance to talk. "Was he a little prince, mamma?"

"No, he was 23 years old. The only son of King Philip and the heir to the throne!" she explained.

"What's an heir?" the boy asked.

"He should have been king when his father died," she explained.

"That's sad," Juan sighed.

His father snorted in disgust. "It is the best thing that could happen to Spain!" he muttered. "Prince Don Carlos was very mad and very bad. If he'd become king we'd have all suffered terribly. I've never been so pleased to put a man under the ground," he spat.

His wife shook her head and told Juan, "He was a poor unfortunate boy." She ignored another snort of disgust from her husband and went on, "Prince Don Carlos's mother died when he was just four days old. He was always a sickly and ugly boy. He was born with one leg shorter than the other."

"The Devil gave him that, Maria," her husband put in. Then he looked up quickly at the saints and made the sign of the cross.

"But it wasn't his short leg or his large, ugly head or his withered arm that was his curse," Juan's mother went on. "It was his cruel mind. He was a wilful and spoilt child."

"Just like cousin Paolo?" the boy asked. He had never liked his older, bullying cousin.

"Much, much worse! And as a prince Don Carlos had so much power to hurt anyone he liked! He often flew into a rage, and when he did he was..."

"A monster," Manuel put in.

Juan was interested, as most children are, in terrible tales. "What did he do?"

"He was a greedy child, for a start. They say he'd no sooner finished a meal than he was hungry again!" Maria said.

Juan looked sadly at the large chunk of bread that was disappearing into his father's mouth and the crumbs that were left for him. "Greed is wicked," he sighed.

The gravedigger spoke carelessly with his mouth full and said, "That wasn't the worst. He liked watching people being whipped. And when he went hunting, if he caught a live rabbit, he liked nothing better than having it roasted alive. If a horse behaved badly then he cut it with a knife so it was lame. They say 20 horses had to be destroyed because of his cruelty."

...d. Cousin Paolo kicked cats when his aunt ...g. "Being cruel to God's creatures is wicked," he

...worst was his temper," his mother told him. "That's o... the seven deadly sins, the priest says. When Don Carlos flew into a temper then no one was safe. Anyone who annoyed him could be whipped. Even lords were threatened. He once said he'd have Estevaz de Lobon thrown out of a window! He would too if they hadn't stopped him!"

"And he *had* to get his own way – or else," the gravedigger said. "There's a story that Prince Don Carlos ordered a pair of boots made extra wide so he could hide a pair of pistols inside them. King Philip told the bootmaker to make the boots the normal size. When Don Carlos saw the boots he had them cut into pieces and then he forced the poor cobbler to eat them!"

Juan nibbled on an olive and was so hungry he could have enjoyed a boot himself, he thought.

"The prince was once riding along a street in this very city when someone splashed water on him from a window. It was a complete accident but Don Carlos had the man executed on the spot!" Maria added.

"Of course he became much worse after the accident," Manuel reminded her.

"That's true," his wife agreed.

"What accident?" the boy asked.

"Ah, that was six years ago," Maria said. "He was visiting a palace, about 20 miles from Madrid, when he looked through a window and saw a pretty girl called Mariana in the garden below. She was just a peasant, but mad Prince Don Carlos wanted to kiss her.

"He raced down the stairs but missed his footing five stairs from the bottom. He pitched forward and struck his head against the door."

"Served the wicked boy right," Manuel sneered. "Don't you ever go chasing after girls, Juan, or that's what'll happen to you!" he said, suddenly angry.

"Me?" Juan gasped and pointed a finger at his skinny chest. But his father wasn't listening. "Cracked his skull, it did. They thought he was going to die, then and there. It's a pity he didn't. It would have saved the poor king a lot of trouble."

"He got better?" Juan asked. "How? You can't recover from a cracked skull, can you, Pappa?"

The gravedigger stretched and sighed and brushed crumbs off his belly and into the grave. "It was a bit of a miracle, it seems. Though why God would want to create a miracle to keep the mad prince alive is a mystery!"

"What happened, Pappa?"

The man turned his gloomy eyes on the boy. "When all the doctors had failed they tried prayers. And then they put the prince to bed with Brother Diego, a very holy ... and very dead ... monk."

Juan shivered. "They put him in a bed with a corpse! Wasn't it a bit mouldy?"

Manuel shook his head. "When Brother Diego died they'd taken his body and dried it out till it was shrunken. It's a bit like the dried beef our sailors take with them on journeys to the New World. It's tough as leather but at least it doesn't go rotten. When they put it in Don Carlos's bed the corpse was 100 years old!"

The boy stared into the deep, dark hole in the floor. "So they put a dried-up monk's corpse in bed with the sick prince? Didn't he get a bit of a shock when he woke up?"

The gravedigger chuckled. "No, son. Prince Don Carlos said that from the moment he touched the corpse he started to feel better. Within two months he was back at the royal palace in Madrid."

"Cured?"

"Cured in body ... but his poor mind seemed worse than ever," Maria told her son.

Manuel spat. "This time Don Carlos made the big mistake of turning against his father, King Philip." The man's large eyes, with heavy dark bags beneath them, turned on Juan. "It is always a big mistake for a son to turn against his father. Remember that, boy."

Juan blinked and pointed at his bony chest again. "Me?"

"Don Carlos got it into his head that he wanted to go and fight with our Spanish army in the Netherlands. King Philip tried to persuade him not to go. Don Carlos said he would go anyway. He threatened to kill anyone who tried to stop him. He confessed to a monk just how much he hated King Philip." Manuel lowered his head and spoke quietly to his son. "Don Carlos was like a mad bull that runs out of control in the bull ring. There is only one way to deal with a mad creature like that..."

"Jump out of the bull ring!" he nodded. He'd seen bull fights and that's what he'd have done.

"You can't jump out of the bull ring when the bull ring is the whole of the Spanish Empire. You have to kill the mad creature before it kills you."

"Kill it?" Juan squeaked. "King Philip killed his own son!"

Manuel clamped a hand over the boy's mouth and hissed, "Not so loud. Everyone knows, but no one speaks it aloud. If Don Carlos had lived to become King of Spain then we'd all have suffered. Our King Philip has done us all a favour. In return we must not accuse him of being a murderer." He released the hand. "Anyway, he didn't murder Prince Don Carlos … not exactly!"

"So how did he die?" Juan asked.

"Six months ago the king waited till Prince Don Carlos had gone to bed. He took his attendants to the room and turned it into a prison. They nailed up the windows. They put a metal fence around the fireplace so he couldn't throw himself on to the fire.

"The prince had heard that a diamond in the stomach would kill you, so he swallowed a ring … but he lived. Then he tried to starve himself and his jailers forced him to eat. He tried to set fire to his bed, but that failed too. In the end, he went back to his old ways of eating huge meals. He washed them down with iced water – dreadful for the stomach. It gave him a fever. He died from the fever."

"His father didn't kill him," Juan said carefully. "But he let him die. Would you do that to me, Pappa?"

The gravedigger looked away. He dropped back into the grave and began to dig. Maria picked up the cloth that had held their meal, rubbed her son's head and smiled. "You're a good boy, Juan."

The boy turned his eyes towards the gloomy pit beneath him. "Would you do that to me, papa?" he said again.

The man leaned on his shovel for a moment. "Shut up and keep working, Juan."

Solve the mystery

King Philip had many enemies. When his son died in the tower of Arevalo Castle they started to talk about murder. They accused Philip of deliberately having his son killed. Some of these stories were just spiteful gossip … one of them may just be true. Which do you think is the most likely?

- Antonio Perez had been King Philip's secretary. Twenty years after the prince's death Perez said, "For four months poison was mingled with the prince's food." If that were true then it could explain why Don Carlos stopped eating for a while. The poison was making him sick.
- A French historian said that the prince had been fed poisoned broth. One dose of poison in the broth killed him – not four months of slow poisoning. But poison victims often show signs of having died that way. And broth is an unlikely meal in the baking heat of a Spanish summer.

- Another story said that Don Carlos was suffocated with a pillow. This would be a good way for Philip to have his son killed. The body would show no marks. Even a doctor would have difficulty telling that this was murder. But the story was told many years after Don Carlos died. It could have been an invention.

- A French historian said that Don Carlos was strangled by four slaves. But, if you wanted to keep a murder quiet, would you use four murderers when one would do? After all, there'd be four killers left alive to talk and tell the world who sent them to do the deed.

- A French writer said that a later Spanish king had Don Carlos's grave opened. When he looked at the skeleton he saw that the head was separate from the body – it was lying between the legs. That meant he was probably beheaded. But the writer was a bit of a gossip and you couldn't trust what he said. Anyway, would Philip want such a messy death with blood all over the scene of the execution and over the clothes of the executioner? The same goes for the story of cutting the prince's throat in the bath. Untidy.

- Don Carlos was starved to death. He was simply left in the tower cell for a week until he died. A simple way to kill someone.

Can you think of another explanation? Here is one that has been put forward...

Prince Don Carlos was a glutton. He often ate far more than was healthy for him. King Philip gave orders that Don Carlos was to be given everything he wanted in his room. With the boredom and the misery the prince could be left to eat himself to death!

It was hot in the tower room. One report said Don Carlos asked for ice to be brought from the Sierra mountains to cool him. So much ice was brought he was able to lie on a complete bed of ice – a pretty sure way to catch a chill. He then ate partridge livers washed down with huge amounts of iced water.

The prince's weak body couldn't cope with so much ice inside and outside. The chill killed him.

King Philip didn't have his son murdered … but if the prince did die of over-eating, it would have been fairly easy for Philip to stop him.

Philip didn't kill his son. But he let him die. What would you call that? A kind of murder?

As long as there have been kings and queens there have been people who have wanted to kill them to get their throne. As a result, there are a lot of suspicious deaths among the monarchs of history...

1. Ancient Egypt. 3,000 years ago King Tutankhamun died mysteriously when he was just 19 years old. A modern writer reckons he is able to solve the mystery of the young king's death after studying X-rays of the mummy. Tutankhamun was murdered with a blow to the head that fractured his skull. The prime minister, a man called Aye, married Tutankhamun's widow and became the ruler of Egypt. He is the chief suspect, of course.

2. Scotland 1567. Mary Queen of Scots was married to Lord Darnley. While she was away from their home in Edinburgh the house was blown up and Darnley was murdered. Most people were sure that Mary Queen of Scots arranged the murder. Mary's letters were found in a silver casket and they seemed to prove that she was guilty. But the letters have disappeared and we only have copies. Were the letters genuine and was Mary guilty? Or was she innocent and the letters a forgery? It's a mystery.

3. Russia 1591. Prince Dimitry suffered from epilepsy and was liable to have fits. It was said that he was playing with a knife in the courtyard of his mother's house when he had a fit. He cut himself and bled to death. A curious way to die! Some people suspected he had been murdered – others believed he had escaped and the corpse was another child. But the mystery was just beginning because 12 years later a young man turned up and claimed to be the dead prince Dimitry. After reigning for a while there was a rebellion in which Dimitry was hacked to pieces and died ... again. Shortly afterwards, a third Dimitry appeared and claimed the throne! He was murdered by a servant while he was out hunting. Third time lucky and this time Dimitry stayed dead!

4. Russia 1825. Tsar Alexander I was not happy being on the Russian throne. He wanted to retire. His own father had been brutally murdered, his favourite sister and his daughter had died of disease and he was miserable. He went off to Taganrog, a small port on the Sea of Azov, for a holiday. The holiday was spoiled by the death of a messenger who smashed his skull in a coach accident. Soon afterwards it was said that Tsar Alexander died of malaria. Or did he? Did the Tsar put the servant's body in the coffin and did he disappear to retire the way he wanted to? We may never know, but there is one important clue. Tsar Alexander's tomb was opened in the late 1880s and again in 1926. Both times it proved to be empty.

5. Germany 1886. 40-year-old King Ludwig of Bavaria was said to be mad, so he was replaced on the throne by his uncle. He was sent to the castle of Berg on Lake Starnberg to be treated. The evening after he arrived he set off for a walk with his 62-year-old doctor. When they didn't return a search was made and both men were found drowned at the edge of the lake. The doctor's hat had come off and it was battered. The king's coat and jacket were found by the edge of the lake. Had he smashed the doctor over the head, taken off his top clothes to swim across the lake and escape – or to kill himself? Had the doctor caught him and had they both drowned in the struggle? We'll never know. It is truly a mystery.

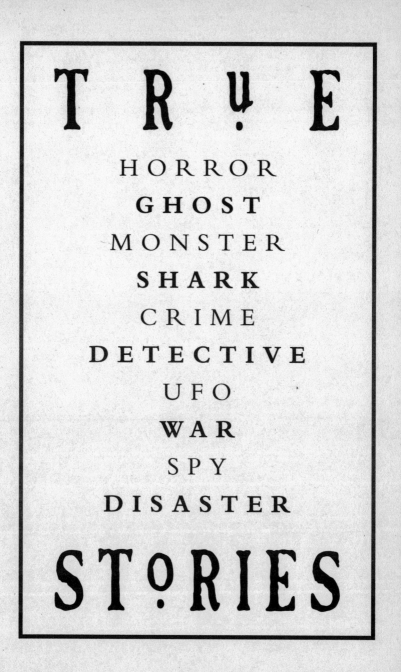

TRUE
HORROR
GHOST
MONSTER
SHARK
CRIME
DETECTIVE
UFO
WAR
SPY
DISASTER
STORIES